CHRISTIAN RAYMOND

HOWL OF THE ICE

This novel is entirely a work of fiction. The names, characters and incidents portrayed in it are the work of the author's imagination. Any resemblance to actual persons, living or dead, events or localities is entirely coincidental.

First edition

ISBN: 9798797091851

Cover art by Sergiu Lupse

This book was professionally typeset on Reedsy.
Find out more at reedsy.com

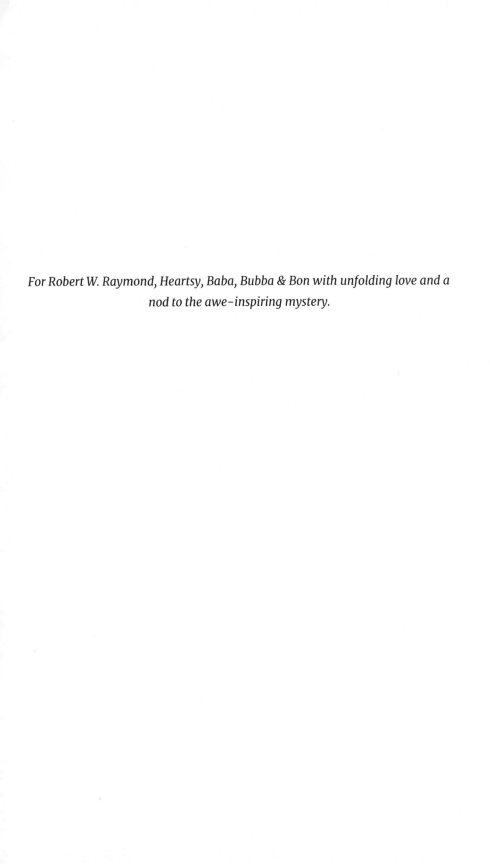

For Robert W. Raymond, Heartsy, Baba, Bubba & Bon with unfolding love and a nod to the awe-inspiring mystery.

Contents

1   THE THICKNESS OF ICE   1

2   NEGLECT BY TROLLS   4

3   OVER THE HILLS   8

4   CHAINS & DRAGONS   11

5   ICE FISHING LIFE & DEATH   15

6   FRIENDLY FIRE   22

7   HYPOTHERMIA VISION   28

8   DAKOTAH & AIYANNA'S SHANTY   34

9   TRACKING ICE   44

10 REALITY OF ALL KINDS   48

11 HOME ICE   50

12 TECH TRAILER   54

13 FROM ABOVE & BELOW   64

14 SHANTY LOGIC, SHANTY RULES   69

15 SLASH'S INSULATED ICE SHELTER   72

16 TELE-SHANTIES   78

17 BEYOND COLD   85

18 HEATED UNCERTAINTY   87

19 THE FISHERMAN'S SHANTY   90

20 ICE OFF, ICE ON   99

About the Author   103

1

THE THICKNESS OF ICE

T he lake beneath Falc's feet let out a gargantuan moan which reverberated in the crisp northern air, blowing and burrowing through his puffy parka to rattle his bones. Piercing, high-pitched popping sounds joined in, like tree trunk thick cables snapping loose on a collapsing suspension bridge. Stepping briskly atop the ice cover, the backpack-wearing fourteen-year-old froze.

Didn't the ice have to be safe for walking on by now?

Creak. Groan. Twang! The lake responded against a gust of howling wind.

Afraid to take another step, Falc adjusted his floppy thermal chook beanie and glared past his hiking boots into the black ice. A frozen field of ice bubbles streamed downward into the lake like inverted, see-through sandcastle drip towers. Myriad squeals, bellows, and twangs erupted atop each other, a cacophony produced from all over the giant ice sheet. *KA-TANG!* Falc's gaze swiveled around, anxiously trying to locate the thunderous cracking speech across the barren, glassy surface.

Breath ghosting, Falc considered his surroundings. Frozen mountain tips enshrouded Blackbird Lake and his tiny hometown of Hillson Falls in Michigan's Upper Peninsula. It was a place so tiny one needed multiple "reverse finger pinches" on a phone's map to even find it. He could see town only a mile away in the valley, a direct beeline across the glassy lake he stood in the middle of on his winter shortcut home from school. Of course, summer would be a different story as far as taking the long trek around the water. But he was all about efficiency.

Mixed feelings on that right now.

Crackle. Clink. Twang!

It suddenly seemed like a very long mile... and amidst the stunning backdrop which he always felt somehow vaguely connected to, like a place he could walk toward forever and never get to. He knew if he needed help, by the time it would come, *it would be too late.*

From up high atop the permafrost crowned Mount Tumbak, Falc appeared as a speck on a pane of fish tank glass, a flick of a finger or tissue away from being wiped clean. He took a deep breath, remembering there was nothing unnatural about the lake "sound effects" as he dubbed them years ago.

Groan! Twang! Pop!

It's just what fresh ice did. Fluctuations in temperature made the ice expand and contract. *That's all, that's it!* His grandpa of course had his own name for it: "Flash Gordon's Laser Show Smackdown" after cheesy sound effects from his favorite 1950s TV show. That fun thought and other nerdy ice know-how didn't change the unnerving, unearthly feeling that the persistent "alien rubber-band popping" imbued in Falc.

The groaning, twanging, and popping escalated.

Falc couldn't help but imagine the ice field filled with Grandpa's old TV show pasty-white "Mars Militia," basically a bunch of guys dressed in goofy spandex jumpsuits and armed with epically terrible plastic guns. They squared off across the humanoid aliens with fake, cheesy prosthetic bumps protruding from equally human actor foreheads. Streams of laser fire erupted and arched back and forth in a volley across the grey sky in Falc's imagination. Figures on both sides dropped and scrambled for position or shelter, the latter nowhere to be found on the open ice.

Falc watched one particularly bony "Zarconian" take a laser shot to the face, head disintegrating from his shoulders on contact. The Zarconian staggered, arms grasping in the air where his noggin once was, before crumbling in a heap on the ice. Sighing, Falc shook his head back to reality. *That was sort of badass but not really helping.*

His attention returned to the lake below. *The ice "sound effects" are all perfectly natural,* Falc tried to assure himself again. While he tended to let his imagination get away, he of course knew that lake ice could be dangerously unpredictable.

So, he did what any sensible person would do. Sprinting, occasionally slipping into a near wipeout, he moved. *Three-quarters of the way across!*

TU-KUNG! A bellowing roar matched his feverish pace. Falc jerked to a stop, catching his steaming breath. In the back of his mind, he prayed that when he stopped, the lake would do the same.

At his feet, sunlight overexposed the translucent ice and what was underneath. *In the nocturnal depths, the vague outline of a young boy was flailing and fighting up through the water toward Falc.*

TWANG-TWANG-TWANG!

Then sudden blackness. Falc struggled to stay conscious, eyes slowly opening and closing, seeing only the ice at eye-level, as if he'd fallen. He was suddenly cold and shivering out of his mind. His body wrenched, the sort of traumatic shaking that meant the end wasn't far off. Had he himself fallen through the ice? *He was wet now... peaceful... floating aimlessly.*

2

NEGLECT BY TROLLS

Alista fought back tears while no-look chopping carrots, using sheer muscle memory in a rustic kitchen. "He didn't know me at all this time," she exclaimed, expression pained. Her thin, forty-year-old figure and long, black ponytail seemed to quiver, even after speaking.

"I'm sorry, hon - we both know it's the Alzheimer's talking. Wish it would get easier. He's just not the person he was before... I wish he were too," Falc's father Bodhi responded consolingly, an ex-city slicker now in flannel and jeans. His square Midwestern head and furry eyebrows focused on her from the oversized oak table. His cinder block sized hands held a chisel over a pile of shavings and an owl house in progress. Such carvings had become a family tradition, starting with Grandpa Rikkar, Alista's dad.

"He said, 'whoever you are, I'm ready to die...'" Alista uttered listlessly. "I just don't know what else to do. He's changing so fast. With what happened to Falc, maybe we've neglected Papa somehow when he needed us most?" Bodhi slipped from his chair to go to her.

Upstairs, Falc was all cozy in his cubby with a nightlight, reading his comic books. Probably the best place to in the house for two reasons. 1) he had a seemingly endless stash of his dad's old golden-age comic books 2) he didn't understand the physics of this, but the cubby (which was basically an oversized closet for no good reason between rooms which he'd long since claimed the floor section of beneath the towel shelving), somehow provided a perfect sound tunnel out the ajar door across the hall and downstairs into the living room for the occasional parental eavesdropping.

This was one of those times. He'd never heard his mom so unsure of herself, struggling to hold it together. Dad was trying to help. This hadn't been the first of these conversations Falc had honed in on.

Falc heard his father, "Maybe we can increase the home aid visits and ours too? Sound good?"

"Or... do we have no other choice now but to move him?

Falc snuck out and into his own room, quietly shutting the door. Static erupted sporadically from a speaker near his computer. Falc ignored it for now as he plopped down on his bed. *With what happened to Falc...* That was months ago. Falc remembered. Sort of. He was found in a hypothermic and frostbitten state, prone in a fetal position, smack dab out atop the middle of the ice-covered lake. It was a stroke of luck he was discovered at all they said, with the usual parental panic, police call, followed by a search.

But it was a neighbor walking their dog who happened to notice Falc's green parka against the ice sheet. Sheriff Chappell was at a loss to explain why Falc was soaking wet and told Alista, "It was like a deluge fell from the sky, but only in a three-foot circle onto your boy. Damndest thing."

There was no evidence anywhere of an ice breach on the lake. No hole, no water, no life-threatening danger. This was only mid-winter ice. Solid as can be. *Solid enough to drive a truck out onto*, which is what they did to pick Falc up and get him out of there ASAP. Local Doc. Bently said he was lucky to still have his fingers and toes considering how fast frostbite nips at the digits. His parents were clearly freaked out by the whole incident. He'd been picked up from school ever since.

At school, Falc had become a bit of a walking urban legend over the whole deal. He was already the new kid from lower Michigan who had moved to the U.P. (the Upper Peninsula) and would never be "Yooper" enough. He'd learned from summers visiting Grandpa (sometimes with Dad), on hunting and fishing trips what that even meant. At least to him, it meant wearing thick flannel, loving arctic weather, eating giant Cornish meat pasties, drinking

5

beer, and basically having an all-around undying pride in being a Yooper by birthright. No, because he was from the lower half, Falc was considered a troll from "under" the Mackinaw Bridge, the dividing line. Zach, the six-foot-five pock-faced near frost giant from his third-period English also kindly noted, "Well technically, you could also go just by Kobald. That would work too." As Falc eventually learned, this was some kind of underground goblin spirit. *Oh well*, he thought.

Falc had managed to sneak back to the lake once (his mom would kill him if she knew) determined to find out what really happened... He wondered whether there were such things as ice hallucinations like desert mirages? Did someone spike his bug juice at school with illicit mushrooms? Falc had decided some time ago there was only one way to find out. He glanced at his bedroom door for security purposes, then clicked on his webcam. The speakers were still delivering some uneven static. The long-range wireless video system tree-cam and mic he'd set up by the lake during his sneak visit captured a limited field of view, image, and audio quality. Nevertheless, Falc stared at the lake remotely on the monitor. No footprints, no impressions, no holes, only a perfectly immaculate layer of black ice.

He kept watching, moving beyond appreciation. He glared, transfixed, not in expectation, but in uncertainty.

"Nothing today, eh?" Falc uttered as if having just another in a series of unsatisfying past dialogue exchanges. Pinned to his corkboard behind the computer screen were scattered papers with titles like "Solunar Tables Schedule" and "Ice Flow Tracking".

Slumping back in his chair, Grandpa ran through his noggin. In his minor obsession with "the incident" Grandpa Rikkar's situation had definitely taken a back seat. Falc flopped back onto his bed, thinking about summers past hiking with Grandpa in the nearby woods. He remembered being about eight or so, Grandpa kneeling at paw prints in the dirt which seemed to magically vanish into the woods. His hands moved over the subtle depth within each impression, unfolding how each undulation revealed a story.

"See the pressure release here and the two-digit turns? It's where she jumped to that bank... right here."

"How?" Little Falc responded.

Grandpa replied, "Just shifted her weight and sprang. She was spooked. Who knows by what? There's a lot of truth in every single print." Falc drifted off into a state of semi-sleep in the memory.

Back on his computer monitor displaying live video of the frozen lake, a silhouette slipped past the camera view, reappearing moments later as it trekked toward the ice. The microphone picked up muffled, conversation-like chatter for a brief moment as the figure vanished into the white distance.

3

OVER THE HILLS

It hadn't been easy for Falc to convince his mom to let him walk over to Grandpa's to hang out for a bit, which before the "lake incident" would have been a no-brainer. He used the old "You don't need to worry about me... I'll go directly there and come right back" routine, which usually worked. It helped that the new home health aide would be there too. Falc recognized his mom was trying to be low-key about her serious concerns. "Just keep in mind he may not quite be himself today. Call me if there are any issues, okay?"

Halfway there already, Falc's feet were already chilly, but he was glad he had bundled up. Zero degrees Fahrenheit wasn't so unusual up there, but the wind chill was a killer. A gust blasted him in the face as he trudged between eight-foot snow mounds on each side of the road. As he leaned into the fresh batch of flurries coming down, for some reason his mind went to just one of many favorite Big Rikkar (as many called his grandpa) stories, maybe because he really needed one about then.

It was family lore from Rikkar's teen adventures canoeing in Canada. While in the woods, Rikkar had stumbled upon a hibernating grizzly bear all snug in his cave. Now, scientifically speaking, you're not supposed to be able to get within fifty yards of said beast without it waking up and being in some serious trouble. In Big Rikkar's yarn, "I crept right up... stealthy as a saber-toothed blenny... and put my hand on its furry brown rump. Just because I could."

8

When Falc first heard this as a six-year-old, he belly laughed uncontrollably; his mom almost had a heart attack thinking her son might someday emulate his hero and try this himself.

Falc knocked on the door of Grandpa's small, snow-caked one-story sectional home, which looked like a pickup truck could chain-drag haul it away at any time. He was anxious to get in as his taste buds fired at the thought of famous Big Rikkar quadruple chocolate hot chocolate. Falc did a small jig, trying to stay warm. He had his mother's circulation, which meant his fingers and toes tended to get cold quickly, no matter the gloves or layers. Angling around a ten-foot-high ice mound left by the morning snowplow, Falc pulled himself up to the window to peer in. All quiet and dark. He knocked again, dreading the idea of having to hoof the two miles back home in the storm anytime soon.

Sighing, Falc meandered around the side of the house, checking in windows. "Grandpa, are you okay? It's me, Falc." He began to seriously worry. Had he been that wrong? Falc realized he'd been secretly harboring thoughts that Mom was exaggerating about Grandpa's state. Heck, he was over for dinner two weeks ago and seemed like the same old Big Rikkar. He even did his terrible patented "coyote politician" joke. Grandpa liked to say he came from the old tundra, the rugged Finnish Northlands, and was always mysterious about possible distant roots to the indigenous Sami. Falc's mom always rolled her eyes at any mention of such. He thought of the reference points for Sami culture in the U.S., which were mostly bad commercials about reindeer herders and gaudy large headwear all used to sell fish. As Falc's dad was part Chippewa, Falc always thought of himself as a bit of an unusual misfit mutt.

He peeked into Rikkar's darkened studio, seeing shadows of familiar wood-carved statues... a snarling polar bear.... a giant writhing salmon... as well as landscape oil paintings of local mountains and lakes. Falc had spent lots of lazy afternoons there, slopping paint around with Grandpa and working on his own comic books. No, not that kind. Unlike 98% of others his age who drew, he for some reason wasn't interested in drawing superhero stuff. For some reason, he was usually drawn toward what was hidden: the background, the minor character no one cared about. He'd write and draw a whole story with

9

foreground characters close up (okay, maybe a superhero or two snuck in) in each frame dealing with something fantastical, but have the story be about the squirrels living in the backyard tree or the awestruck kid in the crowd lost behind a heroic character's bulging muscles. Grandpa loved these stories or at least claimed to. They'd spitball ideas in the studio, sort of a cool little creative collaboration. *When was the last time I was even here?* He was hit with a flood of additional guilt.

Another gust of wind rocked Falc as he climbed the icy back stairs. Through the door, he could see a cup of coffee on the kitchen table. He fiddled with the door. *Since when did he ever even lock his house?* By the sink, he could see a half-eaten stack of pancakes oozing with syrup... A bottle was open with pills scattered about. "Grandpa, are you all right?" came out more frantically than he imagined it would. Turning, he saw fresh tire tracks wrapping directionally around the house. "Oh crap."

Back in front, Falc plodded up to the door one more time. THUNK. His foot rammed up against something wooden. *How did I miss this?* He kneeled down to the snow and ice. A wooden plaque had clearly fallen from the door and was buried. Mixed emotions instantly flooded Falc, literally driving him back a foot to nearly slip backwards off the steps. He dreaded flipping the plaque over. A chill ran down over his already chilled backbone. *Why now?*

He should have pieced it together, not only was Grandpa's car gone which he wasn't supposed to drive - *god help the citizens of Hillson Falls* - but his shanty *was missing from the backyard too! All of which could only mean one thing...* Falc gulped and boot kicked the plaque over, wiping snow clean to read the etched message:

No bitchin', just gone Ice Fishin'

4

CHAINS & DRAGONS

By a frosty pine tree glistening in afternoon sun, Falc squinted across the border between ice-encrusted land and frozen lake. *I don't want to be here.* He thought about the boy under the ice again. Had spent many sleepless nights wondering who he was or whether he was real at all. *I really don't want to be here!* But he was worried about Grandpa. Mom and Dad were on the verge of shipping Grandpa Rikkar off to some nursing home. If he could just talk some sense into him, get him back home, everything would be okay, Falc convinced himself. *We'll be playing Rummikub and slurping hot chocolate before anyone knows any better! So what if he had slipped in a little ice fishing first? Mom didn't have to know everything.*

Falc gave his microphone a final peek, the one he had clipped to a branch up in that pine tree as part of his lake surveillance. *The honest reality here is I'm actually scared of the ice now. No logical reason. Nope. Just pure gut-level visceral fear. Which really sucks.*

He took a breath and tentatively stepped onto the depression of the lake and ice... He could see pockets of frozen "ice bubbles" under the surface, again a sign of solid ice. But his last visit defied logic so he only partially trusted those bubbles.

Falc kept his eyes ahead on the distant mini "ice fishing shantytown," three hundred yards out and smack dab in the middle of the lake. From afar, these could have been small structures set down by intergalactic travelers on a vast, barren Martian landscape. Coming into focus as he moved, Falc made out the tiny ragtag community circle surrounding a pile of wood in a central gathering place with fold-out chairs. Ahead were multiple very humble and large, closet-sized wooden shanties with corrugated tin roofs, which reminded Falc of bathroom outhouses. A fancier FishTech1000 "Insulated Hub Ice Shelter" with its polyester thermal shell and clear plastic windows was off to the side, basically a glorified two-person camping tent. *But where was everyone?*

VRRREEEWWW!!!!! A lawnmower-like engine revved loudly from somewhere close by. Falc caught sight of some sort of trailer unit too, just beyond the shanties. He scanned for the source of the revving, which continued to blare. Falc thought about some of the other lakes in the area and how their Shantytowns could have hundreds or even thousands of shanties by this time of year, overrun with fishermen, not to mention tourists. Up north, ice fishing was a way of life for many people, a subculture within a subculture. It wasn't just a sport, but still sustenance in the winter to some. Each year, ice shantytowns were born again with their own organic "community planning." You'd have new neighbors, ice streets, and activities. The revving grew louder, closer... closer... *where the heck was it coming from?*

Arriving in the ice shantytown, Falc approached the flimsiest structure of them all. Literally built (he knew) from a leftover neighbor's scrap pile of warped wood and old deck, the uneven, discolored plywood protruded in every direction from the eight-by-eight box. The plywood roof angled upward from each side to meet ever so slightly off-center. A jagged three-foot piece of PVC pipe extended from the roof, serving as a makeshift chimney. *Grandpa's shanty of course.*

His old yellow pickup truck was parked behind the shanty, the sort of truck if seen on the side of the road, one would think it abandoned, weeds and brush sprouting from the rusted metal. The revving sound escalated from behind the truck. Falc gaped at a blaring chainsaw emerging from around the truck, wielded by a shaggy-headed howling figure! The figure stabbed the chainsaw violently down into the ice, firing small chunks in every direction before they lifted it and spun in a circle.

It took Falc a moment to realize what he was seeing: a tiny woman in her thirties with giant headphones, dark, flowing locks in a ripped lightning bolt t-shirt (it was 5 degrees out!) and chain waist belt, dancing with her chainsaw. She hadn't even noticed Falc while thrusting the chainsaw about, which seemed to outweigh and yank her about to some spasmodic thrash metal musical beat.

She disappeared again behind the truck. Falc collected himself and slowly followed... watching as she attacked a huge translucent block of ice with the saw, cutting, shaping, and sculpting. She pumped her head in the moment, expression pure ecstasy and agony, as if on a freakishly perfect saxophone riff or in mid concert stage dive. Ice shards spit into the air and frost-covered her face. Behind, several other blocks had been carved into ice sculpture figures.

Chainsaw woman stepped back, observing, then cutting the power in a twirl towards Falc, "What'd you say kid?"

"Ah, hi?"

"That's it? That's all my carve gets out of you?" The banger motioned to her more finished sculpture. "Welcome to my floating wilderness workshop." Falc swallowed hard, collecting himself. He marveled at two incredibly crafted ice sculptures, the first a dragon slinking up from out of the ice; the second some sort of troll-like squat creature.

But it was the third sculpture that seemed to take Falc's frosty breath away. Clearly some mythological creature he wasn't familiar with, its lower trunk was a wide, curved, frozen wave, seemingly levitating in the air from its small broomstick thin ice pole base which defied the laws of physics in holding the beast up. The wave rolled up into a humanoid upper body, with two protruding arms, one pointed up, the other down at nearly perfect ninety-degree angles. Both hands came to deadly spear-like icicle points. *But the head...* was long like a totem pole. The hollow see-through ice skull blended multiple monstrous ice jack-o-lantern-style faces hexagonally. Falc could see two sides, one face with wide eyes and more pointed snout that made him imagine some enraged hybrid humanoid fish carp from the deep, the second a humanoid-hawk visage with an intense stare. Along with the different directions horizontal, another faced downward, and one pointing skyward, an open worm-like maw with two ice fangs. Sunlight reflected through the empty head's translucent ice and cracks, creating the twitching illusion of shifting movement, mixing facial expressions from fear to glee, morphing into each other like animation.

"The name's Slash. What gives?"

Falc nodded back, eyes still on sculpture. "I'm Falc. I'm looking for my grandpa?" Slash returned to her sculpture, brushing away loose snow with a brush.

"The old fart? Yeah, sure, over there. Whoops. Come to think of it, I haven't seen him move since this morning."

5

ICE FISHING LIFE & DEATH

Situated behind his shack, Falc saw his Grandpa Rikkar. The completely immobile figure slumped over a small, round fishing hole cut in the ice which revealed darkened water. Deep cracks and fissures like the frozen lake itself grooved his grizzled face. Rikkar stared blankly past a contraption by his side. A PVC pipe jutted upward from its stand at a ninety-degree angle, reaching over the open hole to secure a fishing rod in place. To Falc, Grandpa seemed embedded in the mountain peaks behind him.

Falc felt like he was disturbing one of Grandpa's paintings. *Was Grandpa Rikkar asleep... or dead? What was he wearing? A traditional Inuit or Sami shirt?* The blend of colorful patterned wool in tie-dye fashion disappeared under his blue jean overalls snapped up over the attire.

"Grandpa?" Falc finally managed to mutter under his breath, now just a few feet away. The ice over the lake had a way of making silence even more deafening and uncomfortable.

"Hello?" Falc tried again. Nothing. *Oh no, was he....*

Rikkar suddenly leaped to his feet. "It's the big one, Wingo, this is it!" The old man jerked on the line stretching down into the fishing hole. "Wingo" was his pet name for Falc, named after a pet hawk he once had named "Wingo Starr" after his least favorite Beatle, drummer Ringo Starr. "Take the rod! Don't let her get away from us!" Incredulously, Falc snatched the rod, but

15

instantly didn't feel any tug. Grandpa tackled over top of him from behind with a gleam in his eye as Falc crumbled to the ice. "She's attacking from the hole behind!" He grabbed Falc's shoulder affectionately, sporting a wide shovel-shaped grin. "Nah, just joshin' but wasn't that a rip roarin' kicker though?" Falc recovered, trying to process how Grandpa could be so feeble and able at the same time.

"Not biting I take it?"

"Not yet."

"Using one of your custom jigs?"

"You bet. Chubby Billy Rattle."

"Ooh. That is a good one."

After the "playing dead" prank, they rambled to the truck, where Rikkar grabbed a thermos from the front seat. Falc thought how good it was simply to see his grandfather, and that at least on first interaction, he seemed like the same old guy from summer adventures past.

Still... he heard his mom's voice creeping in. "Grandpa, you know you're not even supposed to drive. Does Mom or anyone know you're out here?"

Rikkar jiggled his keys in the air with a grin. "Say, want to drive Bessie home for me?"

Falc reflexively jolted back from the car. "I'm not driving that thing on the ice!"

"Don't be such a southerner!" Rikkar insulted him with another label for how hard-core locals referred to out-of-towners or anyone with enough sense not to take a car onto a frozen lake.

"I don't even have my driver's permit yet!"

"Then stay and practice." Rikkar bowed ceremoniously. "I give you the power to walk on water."

Falc sighed. Rikkar always had a way of making things more than they were.

Rikkar nodded to his left. "You must know Aiyana from school, right?

"Aiyanna?" Falc whirled and lost track of his breathing again. Aiyanna Baikie gave a wave from behind the truck, where she leaned over, appearing to tie something up. He could see her furry trapper's hat and long, black ponytail which ran down over her green puffer jacket, almost to her jeans. Falc knew

Aiyanna all right, the 9th grader so naturally original, so naturally everyone's friend, so not-in-your-face real... what "cool" should have meant... and breathtaking... those green eyes... She worked one period a day in the school accessibility office, helping Steve Evins who was in a wheelchair and had motor skill and coordination issues. Falc had that 7th period English with Steve. He'd also see them laughing in the halls and could tell they were close. He usually felt crummy about it, but he was a bit jealous of the time he got to spend with Aiyanna. Her father was a local Chippewa tribal leader, with the family going back hundreds of years to the area's first settlement he had heard. This was of course way before the Finns came across the same frozen wilderness and were reminded of their good old butt-freezing home.

"The only thing that would make this any better would be a little snow," Rikkar said looking serious with a wry grin.

"Grandpa, you don't..."

Please, Grandpa, don't! Falc grimaced in embarrassment. *Not that goofy Snow God Dance Song in front of her! Not that. Anything, torture me, but not that!*

Grandpa Rikkar dove into the polka-style song, doing a jig in place and making his own accordion sounds as he erupted into:

"Time to sing a little tune,
   For snow, not some buffoon,
   I'll add in a little jig,
   As I tie a slip bobber rig,
   I'll yelp and dance on ice,
   Giving it all and being real —"

Falc felt like he was going to die. From behind the truck, Aiyanna joined in, belting out:

"It's the Krunta snow dance tune,
   Remember, Krunta sure ain't no buffoon ..."

Rikkar joined Aiyanna as they roared on together.

"Zellie Krunta snow right now!

Zellie Krunta snow... oh wow!"

Falc grinned and bore a few more verses. Rikkar smiled and patted him on the shoulder before heading out in front of the truck.

"How about a hand, bro?" Aiyanna called to Falc.

"Sure," Falc croaked awkwardly, trying to be nonchalant. He quickly saw she was hooking an old, long, wooden toboggan to a cable on the back of Rikkar's truck.

"What - you don't like snow or something?" she called out.

"No - it's not that, I -" Falc fumbled.

"Must be singing then. I get it. Don't look so stressed, Falc!" Aiyanna smiled, focused on the toboggan.

"Guess, I'm driving then," they heard Rikkar mutter and slam the car door. Falc glared up the length of the truck, masking his mortification.

Aiyanna grinned. "Just hold this." She handed him the toboggan rope threaded through the rolled wooded front. Without thinking, he plopped down and straddled the sled feet first. He felt Aiyanna's legs slide up to his sides, which when you're nine was no big deal, but at fourteen, set off all sorts of reactions coursing through him. Aiyanna patted him on the back with her gloved hand. "Giddy-up!"

Rikkar gave the thumbs up out the driver's window. Falc feigned bravery while thinking how crazy this was as he faked a half-hearted grin. Bessie the pickup truck lurched forward, wheels spinning. The toboggan jerked after, literally built for slick ice. Falc twisted the rope, doubling down on his grip. Aiyanna, held on tighter too. "Wo-yeah!" Bessie pulled them like water skiers, accelerating faster than Falc imagined possible. He gasped at the insaneness of this – watching the truck speed over ice – *how fast is he going, fifty miles an hour!?*

Suddenly Bessie turned on a dime, tires sliding hard right. Aiyanna's eyes widened. "Here it comes! Wait..." She grabbed Falc's hands, taking him by surprise. "Let go!!!" Aiyanna pulled Falc's hands back.

The rope flew into the air as the truck spun away like a stunt car - revealing only what was directly ahead – A GIANT ICE RAMP rising six feet off the ground. "Oh no," Falc whimpered.

They braced into each other – SWOOSH! The toboggan took the ramp full on, like an Olympic luge track turn – propelling them into the air – faces alive with fear and adrenaline in a slow-motion moment all at the same time. They both knew instantly the descent would be – THUNK!!! They ricocheted off the sled, rolling clear of the sled and sliding across the ice in two heaps. Falc grabbed his butt in pain. "I think I broke the butt bone in my left cheek."

Aiyanna slid to a stop. "You don't have a butt bone, dufus."

Later, Aiyanna went back to her shanty to see her father, while Falc and Rikkar approached his dilapidated shanty. "How about we catch us some dinner? We haven't been fishing together in a while." Rikkar gave Falc an endearing side hug.

"Mom would love some fresh fish tonight."

"Was more thinking we'd cook it up here - for the Ice Fishing Shantytown."

"Sure, sounds like a great way to end the day before we pack things up and head home," Falc tested.

Rikkar guffawed as he popped open the wobbly door to his ice shanty. "Want you to see this."

Falc followed his grandpa into the tiny shanty. "Careful," Rikkar said as he pulled the door shut behind him. In the dark shanty, all-natural neon green light instantly reflected off Falc's awestruck expression. An "ice door" in the floor of the shanty had been flipped upward, and beneath, a rectangular child-sized coffin hole had been cleaved into the raw lake below.

The mystical, gleaming water produced more light than the shanty needed or even seemed possible, sending soothing grass-hued shadows rippling up the rotting wood shanty panels, which held richly colored illustrated landscape images. Falc got a whiff of fresh paint. The painted far wall somehow mimicked the field of ice outside with intricate glassy detail, another held a snow-covered arctic forest, the third a moss-colored moon against a star filled sky.

Just as unexpectedly, two trident-like pitchforks hung down from the ceiling a few feet apart, with pointed barbed tips just barely reaching the frigid water's surface. Rikkar touched a third wire which controlled a bobbing bait seen a few feet underwater - an orange polka-dotted wood carved fish.

"Woah, Grandpa, how did you do this?"

"The fish decoy? It's my latest. You should see the ones back home since last you've been over."

Falc felt a tinge of guilt. "Grandpa..."

"But you probably meant getting the ice slab up and out of here, right? Slash helped." Rikkar revved an imaginary chainsaw. "Vroom, Vroooooomm! That's how. She needs the sculpture ice, right?"

By the hole, a tiny monitor screen pack beeped, reproducing a vague greenish underwater view. Rikkar clicked it off. "Sonar depth flasher. Kinda cheating for spearfishing, don't you think? It really just takes a good eye and good listen'n to the water's flow."

Rikkar maneuvered Falc over to a spear, showing him how to handle and push it down into the water. "See? The wire stays connected. You've got to be patient and wait for the fish and just the perfect moment. Then strike."

After practicing handling the spear and its wiring for a while, Falc situated himself over the opening, eyes attuned to the deep. Rikkar sat nearby in a fold-out chair by his sleeping cot and mini-kitchenette, with its single pot and portable space heater. He was snoring loudly before long.

Falc focused for what seemed like ages... seeing a number of fish-like shapes glide by but out of reach through the haze... Then, a large nocturnal silhouette - Falc struck down with all of his might, ZHLUNK! Contact! Falc pulled back, revealing a large beast writhing at the gills, struck cleanly through with the spear.

"First try, that's at least a twenty-pounder, Genius Wingo!"

The fish thrashed wildly at the end of the spear. Falc waffled, just trying to keep his balance against the powerful fish.

"A beaut' of a Northern Pike. Quick in here!" Rikkar flipped open an ice chest. Falc quickly pivoted with the spear, thrusting it down inside. Rikkar gathered up a small handheld bat and with a compassionate nod, struck the fish repeatedly. "Rest easy..."

After Rikkar closed the cooler, for a long while Rikkar and Falc simply slumped down on the shanty floor, mentally exhausted and transfixed by the neon lake glow from below. No doubt Falc thought it had a soothing effect.

"So, everything's okay?" Falc had wanted to ask his grandpa since he got there, as if verification or denial would be the end-all. He had no idea what to do next, whatever the answer. Rikkar seemed lost in thought. Falc continued, "This has been so awesome today, but you haven't been ice fishing in years, right?"

"What are you gettin' at? Sure, I just have an occasional spell or two, who doesn't?"

Falc took a deep breath. "I heard Mom say she's really worried about you. Maybe we should head home now?"

"Oh pshaw. She can't see the big picture out here, the connection between the water, ice, and sky." Rikkar motioned, waving arms and hands in spell-casting fashion. "She, she, she...it's all confusing, but wondrous at the same time, don't you see?" Rikkar took a second, teetering, then rubbed his temples. Falc began to rise to help steady him.

Rikkar suddenly blurted out, "That fish you caught was a big one, but it's not what I'm after."

"What do you mean?" Falc responded, now at Rikkar's side.

"You feel it too, don't you?" Rikkar's wild eyes stared him down.

BANG, BANG! Knocking shook the shanty.

Rikkar jerked up. "You may enter the fortress!"

Slash propped open the door, her locks covering her face. "FYI - We're all meeting up at the fire pit. Even junior's invited."

"Thanks, Slash." Rikkar grinned back.

Falc watched. "Who are these people? How do you know them?"

"Wingo, your mother can't see the big picture out here, the connection between the water, ice, and sky."

"You just said that, Grandpa."

"I did? No, I did not, that's ridiculous! Hah!"

As Falc struggled to mount more questions and the right compassionate response, Rikkar shuffled him out the door.

6

FRIENDLY FIRE

L ater, Falc finished up scaling, gutting, and cleaning their pike on a cutting board under the yellowing twilight sky. The powerful fishy smell triggered more random memories of outings with Grandpa, mostly from summer outings fishing a bunch of different local lakes. Rikkar had taught him how to clean one mean fish to cook up on the spot. He plopped the fillet in a pan and circled the tent to join the others.

The pile of logs Falc had seen earlier was now organized perfectly like a mini-log cabin with a rippling fire emerging from its open roof.

"Won't we melt a hole in the ice?" Falc asked Rikkar, who tended the blaze. Falc propped the pan over the fire.

"Old Inuit technology. The fire is actually stacked and sitting up higher in the hole."

Gathered around, the current "residents" of Ice Fishing shantytown lounged in fold-out chairs. Aiyanna sat chatting with her down-jacket-wearing father Dakotah, the wiry and athletic local English and History teacher who also coached the high school basketball team. He stoked the flames as well with an old fishing rod. Falc caught himself ogling them a bit too much, admiring their closeness, all part of what made her so cool, although he was pretty sure he'd be alone at school in thinking that.

"You have a little Ojibwe in you, Big Rikkar?" Dakotah wryly spoke across the fire.

Rikkar grinned back. "Who knows? Don't do the whole Ancestory.com thing."

Dakotah turned to Falc optimistically. "Good to see you, Falc. How're your stories coming these days?" Falc had him as a teacher the previous year and loved the class. Definitely not so much the composition stuff, but more the creative brainstorming exercises, which involved drawing inspiration from dreams and even stray thoughts.

Falc responded self-consciously in front of everyone, "Hi, Mr. Baikie. To be honest, I haven't been working on much lately."

"Great. Sounds like a creative gestation period," he shined back.

Across from Falc, Slash let out a guttural guffaw, leaning over to Aiyanna. "Is he the kiddo that wigged out on the ice a few months ago?" Slash noticed Falc watching her and realized her elevated audio level. "Whoops. Sorry."

Numerous fish were pan-fried up, shared, and eaten as the conversation continued into the frigid night. Suddenly, a snowmobile roared up, fishtailing to a stop before them and spraying snow dust from the ice across Falc and Rikkar's faces. Falc stared confused at the rising figure in a black rubber wetsuit removing her helmet. Deliza, a tall, gangly black woman in her late 20s jogged over to the fire to put her hands out cheerfully. "What's good all? Don't mind me, just slipping in a bit of research down there. Stellar fire."

The door to the small food trailer-sized shanty popped open and Maple, a linebacker-wide backwoods Yooper with fiery red hair in a flannel pajama onesie and wetsuit visible underneath at the collar, leapt the last few feet down onto the ice. She joined Deliza's side and gave her a peck on the cheek.

"Holy Wah Hani! Just got it uploaded. That is some footage, eh?" Maple excitedly shared in her distinctively Yooper twanging dialect.

Falc took a second to marvel at what wasn't a shanty at all, but he learned was known affectionately as "Tech Trailer" which basically looked to him like a decked-out silver food truck or small RV on the ice. Rikkar told him it was some sort of traveling technical hub for research from Northern Michigan University. Maple turned to the group. "We're not just here to work. Nothing do-een. Got a bunch of lines in too, you betcha. We may be wonks, but ice fishing is in these here bones too."

While Falc was seriously curious as to what they were up to, he leaned into his grandpa and said under his voice, "This has been a ton of fun. But shouldn't we be heading home?"

"I'm not. It's tradition out here to sleep the first night in."

"I hope you're playing. You'd freeze!"

"Nah, you saw my heater. You could stay too, you know. Have a blow-up cot and plenty of blankets. Warm as a slug in a rug. And you know what they say? There's no fishing like night fishing."

Falc glanced over at Aiyanna, who was laughing with Slash.

"Technically, you'd just be sleeping over at my place. We just moved my place here. We've done it plenty of times." Rikkar smiled. Falc considered the day they'd shared, the questions he still had and there was Aiyanna...

He knew he absolutely shouldn't but found himself calling his mom anyways to ask if he could "sleepover at Grandpa's." Of course, like any good mom, she was highly skeptical.

"Give me that. I'd better confirm." Grandpa swiped Falc's phone away, juggling it and nearly dropping it in the fire, others taking notice. Falc cringed, outed and embarrassed as the family drama unfolded.

Grandpa Rikkar held it to his ear. "Big Rikkar here." Moments passed with an occasional, "Yup." Falc nervously eyed Aiyanna. Then, Grandpa wrapped it up. "Yup, sweet daughter of mine, he'll be fine. Yup. First thing in the morning."

Grandpa handed the phone back to Falc, nonchalantly. Falc put it to his ear again. "Mom?" The phone had been turned off. *Had Grandpa talked to her at all?* Falc tried to read Grandpa's expression, who smiled vacantly. Falc came to a realization. *I don't care if it's his Alzheimer's, Grandpa throwing me a line, or an actual "go" from Mom.* Falc had already convinced himself of his own perhaps warped version of plausible deniability. He was going to stay the night.

Back at the fire, the small ice fishing community participated in an ancient ritual: telling stories around the campfire, but with the added twist of being atop seventy-six million gallons of water separated by eleven inches of lake ice, give or take. Slash spun a creepy yarn about ice sculptures coming to life and terrorizing a large ice fishing shantytown. *Go figure*, Falc thought. Maple charismatically told an action-packed tale of a mutated lab experiment at the university, transferring a tiny slug through smartphone technology across the entire student body. Falc also learned what she was doing out there in the first place; Maple was a biologist studying coma or "winter torpor" states, basically as she put it to them, "Why some critters down there under da ice are near hibernating while others are all kinda up and at 'em."

When Deliza's turn came, she didn't tell a traditional story at all, but talked about her deep fascination.... with ice. This actually captivated Aiyanna and Falc as she spun her strange yarn. "For some reason, unlike most stable materials, with ice, every molecule in it spins at a high speed, like one of those fidget spinners on steroids. Would you believe a hundred million spins in a second? It's straight-up hyperactive..." Deliza was downright giddy. "Okay, I'll stop flexing now." Falc was impressed, having never talked to a glaciologist who specialized in lake ice. Many questions came to his mind. Deliza blew Falc and Aiyanna's mind a bit more by telling how white ice expanded upward, while black ice did the opposite down into the depths of a lake.

At that, Rikkar stood and casually squirted a bottle of lighter fluid into the fire, triggering the fire to spike high into the air.

"Grandpa!" Falc exclaimed. Slash eyed Rikkar. "I was wondering where that went. Can I, uh, have my flammable liquid back, Big R?"

Rikkar instead theatrically orated, "You may be familiar with the myth of the Qalupilik."

Aiyanna turned to her dad and blurted out, "I've heard this one! You mean the scary bedtime story you used to terrorize us with? About the rebellious children who can't learn to stay away from the water, and the sea beast that sucks them down into the ocean?"

Dakotah chuckled. "Something like that. Great exhibit at the museum right now on that cautionary tale too."

Rikkar nodded. "That's the one. Exhibit probably right next to one on Wendigo, the malevolent, hungry spirit known to bury itself at the bottom of lakes, waiting to erupt through the water to tear people off their boats and gobble them up. But I'm not gonna tell you about either of those myths or any other Lake Gichigami lore..." Rikkar exhaled as if finished and resumed stoking the fire, which simmered. Everyone looked at each other with a collective, "Well?"

"Grandpa?" Falc finally spit out.

Rikkar shook awake. "Oh ya. There's another one... perhaps an ancient relative to the Qalupilik or a slippery pantheon jumping critter, but much much lesser known: the Jiekna. Purely inland entities bound to freshwater lakes... They lay trapped and dormant in our ecosystem during the summer months. Wendigo? Hah. The Jiekna slaughter them, clean them out as easy as an exterminator wiping his rear. Come winter and the freeze up, the Jiekna emerge to suffocate a community, feasting on our increasingly fragile human psyches..."

For some reason, Falc felt compelled to glance over toward Slash's shanty and the ice sculptures... Through the hazy darkness and zigzagging snow flurries, he could only see a few vague silhouettes now. *Had they melted or fallen back into the ice? Or was his active imagination getting the better of him again?*

"Before the development of our little town, back in the day so to speak, while on my rite of passage, I encountered the very thing."

Aiyanna put her hands closer to the fire, smiling and intrigued by the story. "So, does it pull people under the ice?"

"It doesn't have to." Rikkar glared, expression authentically haunted.

"What's it look like? For sculpting purposes of course," Slash played along, leaning gleefully.

"It's why I'm here right now. I'm going to finish what I couldn't then. I'm going to catch and kill the Jiekna." Rikkar casually continued stoking the fire. Eyes around the fire darted to each other - *was he serious? Is he done?* The fire crackled and popped, seeming to light up Rikkar's intense blue pupils.

Slash was the first to break the silence, "Hah! Rikkar, you totally had me going all crazy old man vibe!" The spell broken, others chuckled at the story. Rikkar responded too, whooping and guffawing a bit over the top, judging by the group's expressions.

"Well, on that epic note, I'll be off to pillage for more raw materials." Slash grinned as she hefted up the spiraling tip of her auger, a long, handheld power tool with a twisted rod of metal for boring holes in the ice. She eyed Falc and Aiyanna. "So, no midnight strolls in the dark outside of the circle, catch my drift?" She motioned down in a drilling motion and made a splashing sound effect. Dakotah slid his chair closer to Rikkar for a more private conversation, openly interested and slightly skeptical. "Amazing, Rikkar. In my grad school folklore and mythology studies, I never heard this one. Can you tell me more?"

Falc watched Rikkar and Dakotah from across the fire, contemplating the story. He noticed Aiyanna was gone. He glanced about... her shanty was still dark. Then Falc noticed Aiyanna sitting alone back on her ankles, back straight, about thirty yards from the fire.

He cautiously approached, straddling the line between concern and invasion. It appeared her eyes were closed.

"Aiyanna, you okay?"

She cocked her head at him, frowning.

"I was meditating. You're not supposed to interrupt someone when they're meditating."

"I am so – "

"I'm kidding! Let me ask you this. Have you met anyone from the 5th shanty yet?" Fresh snow flurries peppered him as he wiped his face and peered into the darkness over the lake. "5th shanty?" Aiyanna nodded and pointed in the direction she was facing. Falc squinted in the moonlight, tilting akimbo and sideways. *No way! After being out here all day, how did I miss this other shanty?*

As if magnetically drawn, Falc stumbled closer for a better view. Somehow he hadn't seen "the 5th shanty" triangulated between Grandpa Rikkar and Slash's shanties. The more rectangular boxed shanty seemed to recede into the icy field behind it, appearing moldy and moss-covered... with dense paneling which in Falc's imagination repelled all light and sound. Flurries seemed to swirl more aggressively around the tomb-like structure.

Falc shook his head at Aiyanna. "Who are they?"

Aiyanna didn't take her eyes off the shanty. "Don't know, haven't seen a single soul come in or out of there yet."

7

HYPOTHERMIA VISION

B ack in the shanty before Falc could ask him about his story, Grandpa Rikkar was snoring like Darth Vader with a head cold. Falc shifted in his sleeping bag and a ski mask on top of a raised cot, quite toasty near the portable heater stand. Rikkar had stretched a blanket across the ice hole to minimize its powerful light, which only worked so well. Questions of the day flooded Falc's mind. *What's really going on with Grandpa? Why did he always feel like such an idiot around Aiyana? Did he imagine the boy in the ice and really just have a weird fainting spell? Who were these people in this weird little fishing community for real?*

Falc shocked awake at 2 a.m. needing to pee in a big way. He snuck outside behind the tent while being bombarded by snow flurries and a howling wind. He relieved himself, exhaling thankfully, while inhaling some flurries. *Something wasn't right.* He angled back around to the front of the shanty... immediately freezing in place at what he saw. Disbelief tugged his boots down onto the ice...

Beneath the intensified whirling snow, Rikkar, Slash, Maple, Deliza, and Dakotah stood in a circle holding hands... completely naked!

The wood-stacked fire was gone. In its place, there was a large, circular hole in the ice which they gathered around... The same mystical green water Falc had seen in Rikkar's tent rippled in the hole, illuminating each of their stoic faces. They gently rocked, either caused by the wind or some sort of collective sleepwalk-like trance. WHHHHHSSSSSSSSSHHHHHHH. The wind wailed like a whisper gone mad, skipping into a screech to hurt Falc's eardrums. He stared at the surreal scene... "Grandpa?" Falc could see Slash catatonic across the circle; her small, stern face was mouthing something he couldn't hear, lips moving at hyper speed. Without taking a single step, the shantytown circle group leaped forward in unison – SPLASH! - They vanished into the sub-zero subterranean waters.

Falc jolted awake on his cot in the shanty, thinking, *What a crazy dream! Wait a second... Where's Grandpa for real?* Grandpa's sleeping bag was wide open. Falc scurried to put on his parka and boots. He emerged from the shanty into the dark dawn – a blast of wind instantly knocked him down onto the ice. On all fours and uncomfortable so close to the ice, Falc hesitated, breath heaving, the fear coming back. The storm had taken a turn for the worst. A full-on snowstorm of dense flakes battered his field of view from black clouds on high. From what he could tell, the logs in the fire pit were still there, but there was no sign of anyone else.

"Hello?" Falc peered around to see the truck; *Bessie was still there!* Bundling up his ski mask, he trudged over to Slash's ice shelter and knocked. *Crickets.* Frustrated, he pounded harder. "Slash? You in there?" After a few minutes, he gently popped open the door. Falc peeked in on an assortment of chainsaws and chisels, a torn Harley-Davidson motorcycle poster, and empty beer bottles, *but no Slash.* Empty cot, sleeping bag ruffled, *just like Grandpa's.* Panic began to rise in Falc. Rushing back outside - WHAM! He ran straight into Aiyanna. They caught each other before slipping to the ice.

"You okay?" Aiyanna uttered over the wind.

"No. Definitely not. Slash, my grandpa – "

"My dad was gone this morning too!"

Falc grimaced. "It's like six a.m.?" He tried to gather himself. *Think.* Falc squatted down, scanning the ice and the thin, half an inch layer of white powder from the overnight snowfall.

"What are you doing?" Aiyanna said nervously.

"No other tracks. I only see mine coming over here and..." Aiyanna

29

interjected pointing, "And mine from our shanty."

"Which means, what? We were abandoned early last night? How does that make sense?" Another gust of wind rocked them both. Aiyanna wiped snow from her brow. "Not just them. I've been to the Tech Trailer; Deliza and Maple are gone too."

"So, we're the only ones here now." Falc pointed to Bessie the truck and the other vehicles. "But how did they get anywhere?" Aiyanna shook her head. "No jackets or winter gear? It's like three degrees out here. With wind chill, probably a lot worse."

"I don't see the weird gag here, even for my grandpa."

Falc blocked snow flurries with a hand, staring across the desolate ice shantytown. Suddenly, the lake felt much more immediate and remote, an expansive and isolated icy wilderness.

Falc and Aiyanna cobbled together a simple plan. After realizing Falc's cell phone was dead since last night (he didn't bring his charger, Aiyanna didn't have a phone as part of her alt-coolness), they found the keys to Deliza's snowmobile in the ignition with some face goggles. Aiyanna found a small notebook with Deliza's name on it.

"Should we....?"

"At this point?" Falc flipped it open. Aiyanna shrugged and helped. They glanced at hand-drawn diagrams labeled "Ice Lattices," showing the order of hydrogen and oxygen atoms in ice. Some were scratched out, others had been expanded and connected to various diagrams. "Maple wasn't kidding. They are both pretty wonky. Let's go."

Bundled up from head to toe in parkas and snow pants, Aiyanna staked her claim. "I'm driving this time." Falc simply nodded, sat down, and grabbed her waist from behind. The not so complicated plan: get to town and find out where everyone went. Falc knew he'd be in it deep when his mom found out where he'd spent the night, but that seemed somehow a smaller blip in his brain now.

As they began out, neither had noticed just how dark the sky had turned, limiting visibility. They started out slowly through the pounding snow and pounding wind, only able to see about fifteen feet ahead. Aiyanna aimed the snowmobile toward town, carefully driving forward. An eternity seemed to pass as they searched for familiar structural shapes ahead: the church tower, a road, the edge of the lake... "See anything yet?" Falc blurted out, teetering on desperation. Frost was forming around both their face goggles. Aiyanna slowed the snowmobile to a near stop. "We should easily be there by now." Falc nodded.

He took off his glove and produced a keychain from his pocket with a compass dangling on it. "Here, we just need to go North." He leaned against her and held the compass in front, so she could follow and drive at the same time. "Good thinking dude." Aiyanna gave an optimistic thumbs up. Falc mustered an embarrassed grin, unused to the attention. With renewed vigor, they scooted off over the ice. Twenty-five minutes later...

"You're reading it wrong!" Aiyanna exclaimed.

"I'm not! Look for yourself!"

"If we keep going, we have to hit shore in some direction, right?"

For over an hour they drove, first continuing North toward town, the exact path (they thought) Falc had walked out to the ice shantytown. It had taken him less than ten minutes to walk from the shore to the center of the shanties. They drove for twenty-five minutes in that direction... The ice continued to stretch out endlessly before them, vanishing into the frantic snow flurries and a vague, dark haze. They tried other routes, sometimes using the compass, sometimes just experimenting. In every direction it seemed, they found a forever wall of icy snowfall.

"We're getting low on gas." Aiyanna worriedly tapped the gauge with her glove.

"This is insane," Falc added, trying to make sense of their predicament.

"Wait, I see a light!"

"Must be a house, step on it!" Aiyanna made a beeline toward the distant light, a sign of something other than snow or the frozen lake was good enough for both of them at this point. Falc was panicking. They just had to get off the ice! They quickly approached... the light growing and coming into view... Aiyanna simply took her hands off the accelerator grips and let the snowmobile drift closer... together they stared in disbelief... the structure came into view...

31

the source of the light, a naked rocker-dude-shaped lamp through a window... of Slash's shelter. They had returned to Ice Shantytown.

After fiddling with the compass and finding nothing wrong with it, they tried two more quick snowmobile attempts, both of which led them back where they started, trapped on the icy hinterlands. More confusion and arguing ensued as neither Falc nor Aiyanna were rookies when it came to compass use.

In Deliza and Maple's Tech Trailer, they rummaged for anything that might help, keeping quiet about the mounting weirdness that had situated them there. Passing the Ice Fishing Flasher screen, Falc halted up. "Did you see that?"

"What, the fish?"

"No, something else. Like a shadow across the screen, but white."

"An underwater white shadow. Don't we have enough issues?

They headed back to Aiyanna's shanty. Inside, Falc noticed how cozy it was, with a pair of wooden beds built into opposing walls, a nerf basketball hoop, along with a mini library with a few dozen books. He recognized a few titles from class instantly, including *Skywater* which he remembered being about coyotes on a mystical journey. A framed map with tattered corners of the Upper Peninsula, circa the 1700s, hung on a wall. Similar to Grandpa Rikkar's shanty, green rays emanated from a circular hole carved in the center.

"My dad's phone has to be around here." Aiyanna scrounged through a duffle bag.

She shook her head, confused, having picked up an upside-down notebook.

"What's wrong?" Falc asked. She stared agape at the pages, shaking her head.

"My dad's journal. I don't understand."

Falc moved closer to try and help.

"Just listen." Aiyanna began reading:

It's 2 AM. Can't seem to sleep. Strangest of dreams. It's the ice hole... it was watching me sleep. As I write this, I'm sure now that it actually was. Is. Like some luminescent, emerald voyeur studying, calling me... needing my assistance, to borrow, but wanting to give back as well. I wish I could describe it as the spirit world, but it goes beyond. When I look into the depths, I see glimpses of... a tiny figure. "Hang on!" I want to say, but my mouth won't agree with me. You must be so cold, so lonely, I'm so sorry... Aiyanna, sleep tight my enchanted daughter. I love you more than anything. I'll just slip into the depths quietly. I won't be long, trust me.

Falc and Aiyanna looked at each other incredulously, then Aiyanna jumped to the edge of the ice hole.

"Do you think?" Falc spit out.

"Oh my god oh my god..." Aiyanna peered into the illuminated greenness.

Falc picked up the journal desperately as if there had to be more.

Aiyanna whirled and calmly grabbed a pair of "Ice claws", a sort of jump rope-looking tool with spear tips on two handles for pulling oneself up on ice in case of emergencies. She wrapped it around her shoulders like a beach towel.

"What're you doing?" Falc watched, sensing the unfathomable inevitability.

Aiyanna was breathing heavily. "Every second counts."

"No way, you can't be serious. It's freezing. Why, why would he have gone in the hole?" Falc asked like he didn't want to know the answer.

Before further protest, Aiyanna gave Falc a determined smile which shifted to uncertainty as she pencil-dived in feet first, vanishing below. He instantly reached down into the water to pull her out.

"Aiyanna? Aiyanna!!!!" He glared into the depths, seeing no sign of her whatsoever. *How could she have plummeted so quickly? Maybe she was stuck up under the ice? I don't want to, I can't do this...*

"Oh come on..." Falc shook his head for clarity, sucking air in short spurts to psych himself up. He grabbed and wrapped the other pair of ice claws around his shoulders. He shuddered in the midst of his worst nightmare, held his breath, and awkwardly tumbled in after Aiyanna. KUR-PLUSH!

8

DAKOTAH & AIYANNA'S SHANTY

The day before, the shanty with faded yellow paint had sat parked and hooked up to a truck trailer outside the high school gym. The sounds of pounding basketballs echoed in the air. Inside on the court, Dakotah wiped sweat from his brow, dribbling the ball in his left hand as two high schoolers converged on him. His mind wasn't on coaching basketball, but rather the weekend he was about to spend with Aiyanna. They'd always been very close, but the separation with her mother had led to a bad argument. He had tried his best, but the reality was... it was simply no one's fault. Of course, Aiyanna was unfairly taking the brunt of it all. He was shocked and happy when she accepted the random idea to ice fish and reconnect.

Dakotah's conscious thoughts returned to the game as he pushed hard left, executing a perfect crossover dribble splitting the defenders, punctuated by a spin move out of reach of the second defender to finish at the basket with a bucket. Dakotah smiled at his students. "If you don't bring the double team fast enough, you're going to get beat every time."

Falc bobbed back up out of the water, gasping for air, elbows extending over onto the ice, being beyond cold, every nerve ending stinging with pain. *Where was she?* He immediately thought while trying to catch a breath, shivering uncontrollably as he finally gulped air. *He had searched underwater as long as he could, which felt like forever...* Teeth chattering, his brain turned over like a blending smoothie. Then he saw Aiyanna up out of the water, kneeling to pull him up. Falc stared at her, still in shock, coughing out staccato, "Saying - again - can't - be - serious?! Haven't you ever heard of hypothermia?"

Aiyanna shot back a confused stare before the shanty door burst open. A furry silhouette aggressively stomped in. Falc and Aiyanna scrambled into each other, joined in mutual shivering. The mysterious figure leered at them, face leaning forward out of shadow to reveal a wild-eyed, grizzled, old man. He was garbed from head to toe in a thick, weathered bearskin. "Get these on and get out here if you don't want to freeze to death." He hurled two similar fur outfits at them.

"Grandpa?" Falc whimpered.

The man Falc thought was his flesh and blood whirled back with the gut-wrenching glare of a complete stranger, before erupting in rage, "Be swift about it! The hunting party won't wait forever. Trust me, you don't want to be left behind." He spun and left.

As their teeth collectively chattered out a macabre song, Falc and Aiyanna quickly stripped out of their clothes. Aiyanna frantically motioned for Falc to turn the other way. "Peeper much? Come on, dude!" Clueless at first, he finally whirled away. "Oh geez, I'm so sorry!" Falc pushed up to the wall, not wanting her to think he was in fact "a peeper" whatever that meant exactly, he thought. They climbed into the anoraks, Inuit garments made from caribou skin, double-layered with fur on the outside and inside to warm the skin, complete with hoodies. They both marveled at the fits and how quickly they began warming up.

"Not sure what was up with your grandpa, but I also gotta find and make sure my papa is okay," Aiyanna whispered nervously as she swept back the tent flap to reveal Rikkar, Deliza, Maple, Slash, and her father all out on the ice in anorak hoodies and mittens, busy packing up a primitive wooden sled with supplies. Each had an assortment of wrought iron pitchforks, whaling harpoons, ice picks, jagged saws, and spears of varying sizes and design, some barbed, hooked or twisted, strapped to their backs. Nearby, several tiny lean-to shelters, constructed apparently from random pieces of driftwood and trees

35

dotted the lake ice cover.

Falc joined Aiyanna's side, mouth agape. "Okay... what? Some kind of weird old-school Inuit cosplay maybe?" Ignoring him, Aiyanna sprang toward Dakotah, almost slipping on the ice. She hugged him. "Papa, what's going on?" He eyed her in confusion before gently freeing himself and returning his gaze to scan the distant ice. "We'll be heading out soon."

"Hello?" Aiyanna said helplessly.

Dakotah turned, considering her more compassionately. "You have a depth in your eyes." He pointed over the horizon. "I need you to look out into the whiteness and tell me when you see anything move." Aiyanna stared helplessly back at him.

"Bring on the new recruits!" Slash roared, looking a bit like a Viking Valkyrie in her anorak, long braided locks flowing out from the sides of her wolf-fur hoodie.

Falc slipped and struggled over to his grandpa, who was packing boxes onto a sled outside the group. "Grandpa, please tell me what's going on? To be honest, I'm freaking out here."

Rikkar gave him a stern look and yelled, "Not your grandpa, boy. Never seen you before in my life. Now step aside before I shove you into the first open hole I see myself, eh?" Rikkar mimed a full-body shiver, glaring at him. Falc waited for the joke, the illusion, the dream or whatever this was to pass, as he hovered in the extended moment, paralyzed. Rikkar's expression grew wilder, larger... Suddenly Aiyanna grabbed Falc by the shoulder, pulling him away as Rikkar strode off to Deliza and Dakotah who were kneeling on the ice, examining the surface.

Rikkar momentarily eyed the two teenagers. "Actually, both of you watch and learn." He motioned to Deliza and Dakotah. "What do we have so far?" Falc could see them studying jagged indentations carved in the ice, long, thin fissures stretched out in multiple directions. Deliza spread out both hands over the cracks, closed her eyes, and took a deep breath. Her eyes shot open and darted about as she ran her hands over the ice, as if reading a coding language. Dakotah walked up and down the fissures, studying various tiny mounds and protrusions in the ice, studying their direction.

"So?" Rikkar inquired.

Deliza opened her eyes, motioning toward a fissure that disappeared into the distance. "Most likely candidate."

Falc and Aiyanna observed, not seeing any differences at all between any of the crisscrossing cracks.

Dakotah nodded. "Agreed. That would take us... to inukshuk twenty-two." He pointed into the whiteout and the empty horizon. Falc squinted, wiping snow flurries from his brow. In the distance, he ogled a hunched shape standing against the otherwise blank ice cover.

"What's that?" Falc contemplated obliviously.

"You dense? Ice inukshuks" Rikkar blurted out disinterestedly.

Aiyanna nodded slowly as if understanding. Falc looked puzzled.

Slash joined them from behind, smacking both Aiyanna and Falc on the back, almost knocking them down. "They're navigation tools made of ice so we don't get lost in a blizzard. Kind of all looks the same out here if you haven't noticed? That one's a polar bear. Carved it my little old self."

"What exactly are we tracking?" Falc hesitantly asked, afraid of the answer he already suspected.

Rikkar chuckled. The others began to follow suit, which swelled into a contagious group chortle at Falc. Rikkar fought back his laugh to go dead serious. "Something you don't want escaping the ice, boy." The hunting party began to move out with sleds, weapons, furs, like prehistoric hunter-gatherers.

Trekking over the ice, Aiyanna and Falc walked in back, each with trident-like pitchforks Slash handed them. They were shaken, dumbfounded, and were having similar thoughts. *How could a dad and a grandfather suddenly not recognize their own family whom they loved so absolutely?* Falc tried to shake off the emotional sucker punch and get practical. Observations flooded his mind. The first was that the shanty they came out of was now the only one he could see out on the ice. *How did the adults remove the shanties so fast since he and Aiyanna got out of the water? Where did the shanties go?*

His next idea he shared with Aiyanna, which was that somehow this was all some group hallucination. Aiyanna doubled down on this idea. "I've read how

Dimethyltryptamine or DMT is easy enough to find in plants like canary grass and can do all kinds of crazy things to people. Maybe it's something they all ate at dinner?"

"They don't seem to have any memory of last night... or us."

Falc tried to feel good about their collaborative arrival at an explanation with some logic, even though it didn't intuitively sit well. *Some progress is better than none, right?* He thought. Maybe she was right; had Slash put something in their fish stew the night before?

Out of the blue, Aiyanna reversed gears on that idea and sighed heavily. "Why are we going there? Let's just face it, we're in some kind of ice fishing hole pocket dimension."

Falc played the naysayer. "It's all bizarre, yes, but..."

She pointed upward. "The sky's clear now, right? Do you see town? Or the highway? Any houses tucked up in the woods? No, nothing but ice every which way."

"Which is basically impossible."

"Best thing we can do is to go back into that ice hole, get back out, and get help ASAP."

Falc shivered at the mere idea. "Hope the hole works that way." He was trying hard not to show Aiyanna how scared he was. He considered what his mom had said about Grandpa and his Alzheimer's. How he had acted like he didn't even know her. His mom had been crushed. Was that what this was? *How many times had that happened to Mom? I should have been more helpful to her. But was this something entirely different, or connected somehow? How did she say to handle it? That's it, have to try to gently bring him back to things he knew, that he could latch onto, that's what he'd do... Maybe it was like that, and I just need to gently jog his memory, shake things up a little...*

What actually came out of Falc's mouth was, "Grandpa, enough! How can you not remember me?" Falc could feel the anger raging inside, heading in the wrong direction he knew. Rikkar and the party kept moving. "Grandpa, stop! Stop right now! Enough is enough!" Dakotah eyed Falc, expression concerned.

Grandpa Rikkar grinned mischievously as he turned around slowly. "Well, you have something to say, spit it out then."

"I am your grandson, do you understand me? Your daughter is Alista, you've got to remember her?" Rikkar aimed back a sly, unimpressed grin. "She's your daughter and my mother for frick's sake! You taught me how to hunt in those woods right out there. The ones, okay, we can't really see right now. Remember your old 47 shotgun? BAM! That kick that knocked me back into your barn once? We've fished this lake every summer since I could walk." Falc stammered, "You... and I've eaten entire tubs of homemade ice cream together!"

Falc grasped for memories, running out of steam. "Remember the time with the big tub of Blue Moon when we both threw up all over -" Suddenly Rikkar leaped in the air, defying his age, landing an inch away. His instant proximity was enough to knock Falc back on his butt. Rikkar knelt down and grabbed Falc by the collar.

"Listen, boy, I said you were mistaken. Call me Grandpa again, and I'll feed you to it myself. And it's Rikkar, eh?"

Falc fought back tears and a whimper, searching the man's eyes for any recognition, sending puppy dog-like oxytocin at him in a last-ditch effort to connect. Cold, angry eyes stared back. It was the gaze of obsessed men throughout history, without time for pleasantries, let alone family. Falc exhaled a fearful breath. Under him, he noticed a wide, jagged crack line jutting along the ice between his feet. "Do you see that?" Rikkar stiffened, head darting about as he yelled, "New Track!" The rest of the party halted into a crouch, searching the ice. Rikkar put a finger to his lips for Falc; he bent down listening closely... then stood and sniffed the air. "False alarm, not them... yet."

"Them?" Falc questioned, which was left hanging.

Dakotah scanned the ice nearby. "We better be off." They kept tracking. Falc pulled into himself. Aiyanna watched worried as the day and the drudgery seemed to drag on. She spoke softly, "Listen, we're going to figure whatever this is out and get everyone back home, okay?" Falc gave her an appreciative half-smile, trying to shake off his malaise.

A bit later, Falc worked a new angle. He trotted up alongside Slash. "Excuse me, ah, Slash?" She gave him a momentary glance, not breaking stride. "So, where are your chainsaws? Can't be without those." Slash shot him a peculiar look as if struggling to grasp a distant memory, then tried to pronounce the seemingly exotic word. "Chain-saaw? Don't know what you mean, but I do like the sound of this word." Falc continued, "Are we some kind of chosen ones in all this? Like in a prophecy?"

"Chosen ones?" Slash guffawed and slapped her knees. "More like human sacrifices!" Falc and Aiyanna exchanged grave looks. Slash gave a sly look. "If you're lucky that is. Don't stress though. If you survive the first day out here, you've got a chance!"

Further ahead, they came upon slushy snow drifts staggered across the ice. Falc looked down into the black ice as they moved, which had a nearly hypnotic effect. The ice seemed to move under him, then speed ahead, making him dizzy. He quickly realized what he was seeing: an enormous, turquoise-colored fish, scales reflecting almost metallically, swimming directly below him under the translucent ice. Falc halted and stared in awe, as if through a glass-bottomed boat, as he reached to tap Aiyanna. After a few seconds, its tail finally sashayed past.

Falc went pale. "Seeing this?"

Aiyanna nodded, saying more loudly, "Is that what we're hunting?"

Rikkar glanced back in their direction nonchalantly.

"Harold? Don't worry about him, we got bigger fish to fillet."

"But... it's like the size of your truck!" Falc tried to stay calm.

Rikkar kept moving ahead. "What did I say about holding it together?" Maple rushed back to them. "Could be they're a sign of good luck for you. Did you see which way my big baby got on to, eh?" Falc pointed. She cheerfully patted her satchel tied to her waist. "Next time, have some meat pasty bites for her."

As the march unfolded into hours, the sky grew grayer, adding to the bleakness of the vast wasteland. Aiyanna and Falc hardly noticed as they considered options. She attempted to talk to her dad again too, with little luck. Dakotah kept his responses limited, ending with, "Your training will come in handy, trust me." Falc went out on a limb and told Aiyanna about that day on the ice: the cracking ice, the boy under the ice, and being knocked out. He left out the gory details about his new-formed ice phobia but had the feeling she could sense it. Falc hadn't told anyone at school the story, so he knew what it could mean as far as things getting around, but somehow now, none of that seemed to matter anymore. Somehow Aiyanna seemed intimately trustworthy to him. She simply responded suddenly shyly, "Thanks for telling me. One way or another we're gonna find some answers to all of this, right?"

They noticed Rikkar kneeling on the ice up ahead... He was examining a fishing line attached to a wooden stand over a small opening, a similar-sized hole to the one Falc first saw him fishing when he arrived at the lake.

"Maple, can you please tell us exactly what we're fishing for?" Falc muttered.

"Now, hon, you telling me for real you don't have a clue?" Maple shook her head.

"It's all about the lures," Slash pitched in cryptically as she dug into her satchel, producing two small human statues, one of ice, one carved out of wood. "I did the ice, Rikkar the wood. We need to bait those additional holes over there." Falc gulped.

Creak. Groan. Screech.

Falc and Aiyanna froze, listening to the worrisome lake exhalations, while the rest of the party continued on nonchalantly. "The ice is getting thinner. We're close," Rikkar uttered solemnly. Falc looked at Aiyanna. "That's a good thing? What are we doing?"

Creak. Groan. SCREECH!

Rikkar halted, raising two fists, instantly stopping the party in place. Falc and Aiyanna glanced over the barren ice, Falc freaking out at the familiar sounds. Rikkar whipped his head to him, wild-eyed. "Listen." Falc literally leaned an ear forward... hearing a low rumble in the distance... growing louder.

Creak. GROAN. SCREECH!

Aiyanna muttered under her breath, "Is that someone screaming for help...?"

"Or is the ice?" Falc responded.

"Is there a difference?" Rikkar scanned the ice.

Thunderous cracking sounds came at them from multiple directions. Falc whirled, looking for hairline cracks in the ice. The lake cries suddenly escalated, growing shrill and multiplying, a painful chorus tearing at the surface. GROOOOAN! SCREECH! GROOOOAN! SCREECH! Aiyanna and Falc covered their ears. Falc leaned into his grandpa. "What's happening?" Rikkar yelled into his ear, "It's the KEENING."

"The what?"

"The cries of those already taken... which means *it's* close. Our mission is clear." Falc and Aiyanna exchanged worried looks. Falc gripped his pitchfork. *Was the boy trapped under the ice one of the "taken"?*

"You're saying there are ghosts under there?" Aiyanna blurted out. Suddenly, jagged cracks emanating from a hundred yards away shot across the ice at them, hurling through their legs, around, and past them.

"SCATTER! GET BEYOND THEIR REACH TO SOLID ICE!" Dakotah screamed. Like geysers, exploding holes of ice and frigid fluid erupted upward across the frozen minefield, spraying fractured ice sheets. "Watch out!" Deliza sprang clear. The disjointed party chaotically tried to maneuver clear of rupturing holes and bombarding ice chunks, Maple and Deliza separated by a gaping jagged hole.

Aiyanna tumbled forward away from a new fissure, and into a handstand, flipping completely over and managing to land on her feet. She leaped and somersaulted around another hole. "How?" Falc exclaimed, amazed and terrified while sliding and trying to maintain his own balance. "Mom made me take gymnastics until the 5th grade. Hated it... until now." She motioned to Falc. "Come on!" As they tried to run, the ice shook and moaned directly beneath them. They dove in opposite directions as a burst of ice detonated between them to form a new crater. Ice holes blasted upward left and right, showering down dangerous shards of ice and freezing lake water. Rikkar stabbed his spear down into the water of an open hole. "Everyone get clear!" Slash and Dakotah deftly maneuvered around ice explosions, fending of shards.

A flying chunk of ice clipped Falc, knocking him down and inches from an open hole! Stunned, he stared into the black water... A vague image of a young, brunette girl began to rise toward him from the depths... but her dimensions were all wrong as she spun upward... her entire body a thin layer of jointed white ice. Like a back-projection TV or mirror... she rose with a melancholy expression, reaching upward... her phantasmagoric form accelerating through her life cycle, from girl to teen to woman to crone and back to baby again... she approached, about to break the water's surface...

"Falc!" He snapped awake at Aiyanna's voice and rolled away. Aiyanna was twenty feet away on what appeared to be solid ice. Closer in, Maple pushed Deliza to safety from cracking ice, then leaped over a hole. "Cripes almighty!" On her descent, Maple landed directly over another explosion of ice! She instantly submerged into the surging, frigid water amidst the shattered ice, her hand making a futile grab for an edge before vanishing.

Water sloshed up over the ice cover as holes continued to mushroom like a minefield around them. Rikkar shot across the ice on his knees, going headfirst, groping at the black water which had swallowed Maple. Falc and Aiyanna gathered themselves in the distance. Rikkar's soaked upper body emerged, dragging Maple's form up onto the unstable flow. "Slash, fire now!" Dakotah scooted over to Rikkar and helped bring Maple to her feet.

"Now I'm just fine, I'm fine..." Maple incoherently muttered, shaking uncontrollably. Deliza staggered around a hole to get closer. Maple reached for Deliza's hand. In return, Deliza used both her hands to rub warmth into Maple's, blowing into it and watching her carefully.

Slash went into high gear. "Over here!" She skated between two fresh holes, water sloshing up onto the ice cover. She leaped over another hole, landing in an area free of cracks near Falc and Aiyanna. Removing a glove, she revealed a tiny, hidden, smoking red ember hidden in a seashell, which she softly blew into. "Come on, baby." From her backpack, she dumped logs and tinder onto the ice, quickly working to start a fire.

Arriving and trying to help, Falc went down on a knee to arrange the wood.

Rikkar slid Maple over and produced another dry fur from his backpack. He turned to Aiyana. "Help me get her clothes off. If you don't get her in something dry and by the fire soon, she's done for." Maple gave a thumbs up and stuttered, "Thanks, R. That first step's a slippery one." Deliza nodded.

"The attack is over though, right?" Falc hoped.

"Hah. Those baby holes are the least of our worries."

43

9

TRACKING ICE

L ater at the flickering fire, Maple wore the dry furs and perked up from her frigid delirium. "Come on, I'm fine. Got to get da game face on now..." The storm had picked up, whipping winds adding to the persistent snowfall. Slash passed around pieces of fish jerky to everyone which they chewed on. A blast of wind hurled snow flurries across the arctic tundra, causing the party to lean in to protect the flames. Aiyanna heard a steady grating sound and glanced into the maelstrom... Across the potholed icy battlefield, she saw a figure fifty yards away in distance. At first, she mistook it for a person, but then recognized it as ice. An ice sculpture.

"Is that... another inukshuk?"

Falc saw it too and tried to convince himself, "For navigation. Has to be right?"

Rikkar pivoted and stood, raising a whaling harpoon in one hand, a barbed, 8-tipped pitchfork in the other. He exhaled slowly, not taking his eyes away and uttered, "The Jiekna."

Falc squinted through the flurries, using his hands like binoculars. "Slash's creepy sculpture? How did it get way out there?" Slash eyed Falc, not understanding the comment. Rikkar's expression intensified. "Get armed."

SSHHHZZZZZT! The ice sculpture dropped and vanished into the white ice. Falc gulped. "It went under the ice?"

"Nope," Rikkar retorted, eyes focused ahead.

"Then where?" Falc asked, concern growing. Rikkar simply grunted back.

Slash shook her head. "Name translated means... The Ice."

"Believe what's in front of you. Heat em' up." Rikkar stuck both his tipped weapons into the fire; everyone followed suit. With smoke-tipped gleaming hot metal, Rikkar directed the hunting party into a back-to-back circular formation to cover every direction. "When it's directly below you, it's vulnerable for a split second." Falc glared down through the black, transparent window of ice. Aiyanna and Falc exchanged completely vulnerable, terrified looks. The teens stared ahead tensely through windblown snow, visibility next to nothing, imagination turning every twirling flurry into a potential attacking monstrosity.

"Come on you bastard..." Rikkar focused to his right fifteen feet away. "There!" Falc and Aiyanna saw it for a split second, a shimmering outline actually inside and part of the black ice, a glazy jack-o-lantern-style hawk face uncannily peeking upward while gliding fluidly toward them, now forty feet away. Its head spun to other crystalline humanoid facial versions, protruding glimpses of coyote then a bear snout. Arm-like appendages with mangled frost claws propelled closer through the ice cover...

Rikkar cocked his harpoon back; suddenly the ice buckled beneath them like a rug being shaken from one end. The harpoon jostled off-target, clanking across the field. The party was hurled across the ice. Falc scrambled to his feet. An icy spike shot up from the ice cover, catching his furry sleeve and grazing his arm as he winced. Falc managed to rip free, leaving his sleeve behind, and eyed a bloody arm gash. Rikkar wildly stabbed his pitchfork at the ice, mostly achieving little penetration as it bounced back upward. "Face me! Where are you?"

Slash crouched with a dagger, cautiously moving in a circle. Behind her, sliding horizontally along inside the ice, the Jiekna's frozen twisted head crept closer, bestial ice faces glaring in every direction at the same time, including upward... as it approached her feet. A claw of ice slowly emerged... and grabbed Slash's ankle! She wailed angrily and unsheathed a saw-like sword from her back while being yanked off balance to slam onto the ice. Her sword skittered away across the ice. A few feet away, Aiyanna saw the action and let out a battle yell and lunged. "IEEEEE!!!!!" She stabbed the claw with her spear. Heat sizzled against frost, causing it to retreat back into the ice. Slash gave a thankful nod to Aiyanna and grabbed her sword as an ice spike shot up, missing her face by a millimeter. Dakotah and Deliza were both still on all fours on the ice, recovering and escaping near falls into holes. Dakotah yelled a warning, "The Keening is in full swing! Don't let them take you!"

Nearing the fire, Rikkar gathered up an ice pick and continued attacking the ice haphazardly, a wad of drool flinging from his mouth. "I'm the one you really want, come on!" Maple squatted on the other side of the fire, still shivering, harpoon in hand. She sensed danger, eyes darting side to side. Tentacle-like ice claws rose up, flanking her. Three feet in front, the Jiekna's hollow head rose slowly, revealing the figure of melded ice, one visible face hawk-like, the other an iced little girl's face in the shape of morphed tree branch-like icicles.

Twenty feet away, Falc saw Maple's predicament; Rikkar was closer to her but seemed oblivious as he rambled on, madly randomly stabbing at the ice. "Have at it demon!" Falc pointed to Maple and pleaded as he tried to slide closer, "Grandpa!" Rikkar, in a berserker rage, face crimson, kept at the ice. "Face me!"

Expression horrified, Maple began to backpedal, slipping away from the Jiekna's hawk face. Falc moved in, still too far away, running, pointing, screaming..."Grandpaaaaa, Look, Maple!" Reveling in his rage, Rikkar continuously rammed his pitchfork hopelessly into a fissure.

Maple kept backpedaling, not seeing an ice sheet rising behind her...

"Some humdinger..." Maple suddenly lurched in one motion, bare-handed, grabbing a piece of flaming firewood and hurling it at the Jiekna's head. She grunted in pain, burning her hand. "Try this sucker!" The Jiekna dodged left, the flaming projectile flying harmlessly past.

The ice sheet pulled up behind her, halting any movement... Suddenly entrapped on all sides, head, claws, tail.... Maple gulped in abject fear. The top of the Jiekna's head cracked open. The gigantic worm-like maw head suddenly dove forward from the ice, spinning onto her like a four-sized buzz saw, and

46

sucking her feet first, swiftly, fluidly into its hollow head. It quickly melded away back in the black sheet with Maple, leaving only windblown flurries over the empty ice.

10

REALITY OF ALL KINDS

Back at the campsite in front of Aiyanna and Dakotah's shanty, the group huddled around a fire as twilight gave way to darkness. Slash comforted Deliza, who was fighting back tears as she stared blankly into the fire. Aiyanna tried to persuade everyone to leave the way she and Falc came. She tried to explain how supplies could be brought back to help them too. The idea was instantly shot down as "impossible" by Slash and "against our mission" by Rikkar. Dakotah sat quietly, seemingly in deep contemplation, occasionally looking at Aiyanna, as if confused. Falc could only shake his head at the apparent collective amnesia, thinking of Maple now... *and Grandpa.*

For a long while, they sat in silence around the roaring fire. Night had fallen. Even with the fire, most of the party shivered. Even through his hoodie, Falc's ears hurt and felt frozen as he watched Rikkar and Dakotah across the flames, talking strategy for the next hunt. He hardly realized Aiyanna whispering something to him as he tuned out, his focus and escalating rage on Rikkar... Finally, Falc stood.

"You just let her die."

Rikkar turned from Dakotah, seeming to address the fire rather than the boy matter-of-factly. "It was just her time, nothing more, nothing less."

"That's awfully heartless, isn't it? You were right there. I called out to you, and you did nothing. You could have – "

"So quick to judge. How did you react when you were needed?" The words cut Falc to the bone, resonating beyond the moment. "What do you mean?" Rikkar continued, "I'd imagine you'd be trained better than this, for such situations. I guess not. Maple was the best of warriors who will be missed and honored, eh?"

Anger boiling over, Falc never felt so helpless as his temper teetered on exploding. Aiyanna put a hand to Falc's shoulder, softly whispering in his ear, "Let it go, there's no point." He looked at her, fighting back the mixed emotions and tears. She motioned him to follow her. Rikkar called after, his tone more compassionate, "Not ever safe to go through the da lake ice again, if that's what you got to thinking. There'd be consequences for that."

Inside her shanty, Aiyanna quietly closed the door. "Look, there's nothing we can do about Maple now. I think we do need to try the ice hole portal again, regardless of what your grandpa - Rikkar - says. See if we can get some help to end this insanity." Falc could only nod. *Grandpa was somehow talking about me, unconsciously without knowing...* Falc tried to focus on The NOW. *Does the portal door swing both ways? We're about to find out.*

They heard voices arguing outside, drawing closer. "We need to hurry before they try to stop us!" Aiyanna was already taking her furs off as Falc came out of his daze, accidentally staring directly at her partial nakedness. "Hey, peeper!? Do you mind?" Aiyanna covered herself. Falc turned away. "My god - I'm sorry again, sorry!" The shanty door was being jostled.

"See you on the other side?" Aiyanna said hopefully, hugging her arms over her front side. Focused squarely on eye contact, Falc tried to offer a confident nod. He whirled to see Grandpa Rikkar lift his pitchfork angrily toward him as the door opened.

Aiyanna took the frozen plunge into the ice hole SPLASH!

11

HOME ICE

"Put these on fast." Aiyanna passed Falc a towel, a pair of her dad's jeans, a turtleneck, and a sweater. He shook off a shivering nod, a few seconds removed from the ice hole and back in Aiyanna's shanty again. The old wilderness map nailed to the wall caught his gaze as he hurried to dry himself, which wasn't there through the portal on the other side. The pre-portal entry moments prior rushed through Falc's mind. He had managed to dive into the portal as Rikkar lunged to stop him. *What would Grandpa have done? Would he have really hurt me? Was he even Grandpa anymore? Could a place be infected with Alzheimer's?* When Falc had returned, Aiyanna had already been dressing and had helped heave him up out of the frigid water. Warming up from that kind of bitter cold was a process and not an easy thing to do, he had learned. Falc glanced at the small digital alarm clock on the table, which read: "7:03 a.m."

"We've only been gone an hour?"

"Yup. Roll with that too."

While dressing, a distant... "Beep Beeeeep..." directionally turned their heads. They shared an optimistic glance as Falc hurriedly yanked the sweater down to his belly.

Pushing outside, the storm had cleared enough to see through a thin mist to the road: an SUV drove off in the distance. Falc's eyes scanned the ice... *all of the shanties were there! But still no sign of anyone... no Grandpa.* He eyed the shoreline. "Let's go!" They sprinted, hand-in-hand for steadiness on the ice. CRACK-ITY CRACK! Aiyanna's foot shot through thin ice down to her knee.

She eyed her submerged leg as Falc helped her up. "What happened - since yesterday? Heard of climate change, but..." They both knew somehow in their guts; somehow what happened through the ice hole portal was hyper-accelerating the early ice melt in their world. Then he saw it. *So much for any idea this was all some sort of group hallucination,* he thought. Thirty yards away, a faint glimmer of sunlight revealed the shimmering, vague outline moving in the snow-covered ice, speeding like some fantastical ice shark straight for them! *The Jiekna.* "Back inside!" Falc and Aiyanna ducked back inside the shanty.

"It somehow followed us?" Aiyanna gasped.

Something was different about the shanty as they entered: the overpowering green light was gone. They stared at the hardened ice in a joint realization. The ice portal, their entry and exit point to the phantasmagoria where their family and new friends were banished, had completely frozen over in a matter of minutes since they had left the shanty. "I guess it's a one-time round trip-ticket only." Falc touched the perfectly sealed ice as if to make sure it was real, wondering if he'd ever see his grandpa again.

Aiyanna nodded. "Right, and we need to worry about that thing out there."

They peered out the shanty door, checking for the Jiekna. A wind gently blew. "Is it hiding?" Falc whispered. Moments later, they burst out of the shanty and made a beeline to the nearest structure, the Tech Trailer. CRUNCH. CRUNCH. CRUNCH. The sound of their every step against the packed snow felt amplified as weary of slipping, they tried to jog quickly while scanning the ice cover.

Relieved to arrive at the door, they glanced back one last time. Eerie silence. Falc pondered the ice. *How DID the "Jiekna" get here? Maybe killing Maple gave it some limited access to our dimension?* They pushed inside the darkened Tech Trailer, which seemed spacious. "Here it is." Aiyanna found and flipped on the lights, illuminating monitors, scanners, topographical maps, and scuba gear packed inside.

Falc jerked back screaming, "IEEEEIIIIAAAA!" Maple's body lay there, prone on the icy floor, next to an almost coffin-shaped rectangular ice hole. The same green light as Aiyanna's shanty cast neon shadows across Maple's seeming corpse and the trailer. Maple's face had a grey hue; her entire figure was covered in a thin layer of frost. Aiyanna joined Falc, checking for a pulse on her wrist. She pursed her lips, trying not to panic. "Can't find it."

He racked his brain for answers. *She was taken by the creature, but she ended up back here?* He suddenly remembered something. "This may sound crazy... but maybe she's like in a torpor state? Some frogs hibernate and freeze solid, except for the insides of their cells. Turtles out here go without breathing air for six months at the bottom of the frozen lake..."

Aiyanna frowned. "She's not a frog or turtle!"

"It's just actually what Maple told me at the fire last night."

"You know CPR?" Aiyanna said, trying to bring the conversation back to reality. Falc nodded. Aiyanna motioned to him, and he straddled Maple, beginning chest compressions, while she blew in her mouth, lips so frigid to the touch.

"Again," Aiyanna said pragmatically.

They continued for another ten minutes, chest, mouth to mouth, and listening for breath, but to no avail. They eventually flopped back in silence, defeated, simply staring at her immobile figure. After a while, Falc rose and began rummaging around the trailer.

"What are you doing?"

Falc opened a closet, pulling out a wetsuit and holding it up to himself. "Got to prepare to go back in."

"What do you mean? What about Maple?

Falc began putting on the wetsuit. "I wish we could help her, but it's possible the best way we can if at all possible is going back in. Maybe the fishing hole in here will lead us right back to the group."

"Or... we could try to sneak past it - the Jiekna - get help. Get off the ice."

"Assuming we make it. My parents are bound to call the sheriff when I don't come home this morning."

"Could be hours before they find us."

Falc exhaled earnestly, a visceral gut feeling rooting him to the icy floor. "Look, I don't know about you, but I'm not leaving my grandpa, your dad, or the others behind in there if I can help it." Falc pulled out another wetsuit, checked it for size, and raised an eyebrow to her.

"Can't hurt to take a quick dip in the wetsuits to see, eh?" Aiyanna grinned, trying to sound convincing. Falc snapped the rubber around his face snugly and gulped sheepishly. "This time, how about I go first?"

12

TECH TRAILER

D ays earlier, the "Tech Trailer" or Mobile Research Center had been positioned outside the campus science center. Maple passed by it heading to meet Deliza, who apparently was ecstatic about something she'd come up with in the lab. It was also going to take them out into the field, which Maple positively loved, and she softly uttered out loud, "Da lake." They could use some good news like that after the previous night's blood sport. Visiting Maple's parents was always the case, considering her homophobic-racist combo dad and bro. But Deliza was always of the same mind that they'd visit for Maple's mother and to show they were both tougher than nails when it came to body-slamming ignorance.

It was a sad state of affairs, but it kept them from getting soft and "cocooning" too much outside of reality. Maple's brother, who was a security guard in a local jail, was a particular piece of work who liked to brag about using his gun and beating up inmates. Some of Deliza's stories about growing up in Detroit usually shut him up pretty quickly. Maple couldn't wait to see and hear what Deliza had come up with as she pushed through one side of the lab's double doors...

Falc emerged instantly from the icy waters to flashing monitor lights and overheard arguing. He planted his elbows upon the icy hole's edge, kicking his feet horizontally in preparation to crawl out... when Slash, in a wetsuit herself, tugged him out by the arms. "Up you go!" She quickly handed him a towel. "Thanks, Slash," Falc muttered, never taking his eye off the hole, focused on Aiyanna. *Where was she?* Seconds seemed to agonizingly elongate. A hand broke the surface, Aiyanna emerging in her wetsuit. Falc quickly took her hand to help with the climb out, her wetsuit pouring water back into the hole. Slash began to leave through a curtain a few feet from the hole. "Ready to rock n' roll, eh? Throw on those jackets over there and come join the jam when ready."

Falc moved to peek beyond the curtain, catching images of the Tech Trailer. Deliza, Rikkar, and Dakotah were garbed in the same university-logoed wetsuits and stood at a wall-sized monitor, examining an underwater bathymetry map, which revealed the lake's contours and depths, identified with brightly hued greens, blues, and reds in 3D. Nearby, smaller sonar depth finder screens were marked with various location "spottings." Falc pulled back the curtain.

The whole scene felt to Falc like he was in an ice fishing crime scene investigation command center. Aiyanna marveled at the site too as she wiped her face. "So...?" A quick whispered conversation assessing the possibilities followed. They clearly weren't back with the hunting party they had left, or still in their own world where they'd started. *This was somehow different than either.* There was no way everyone could have gotten inside the Tech Trailer in that instant they came in and out of the ice hole.

None of the "tech ops center" was up and running before they left, and there were systems here they definitely hadn't even seen back in the darkened trailer before they left. Were the adults "acting out" this whole thing for some reason? Why possibly could that be? To teach some lesson? Back to the portal possibility, Aiyanna mused that maybe each shanty was an entry to some alternate reality somehow combined with group hypnosis? All they could do now was investigate further. They entered the main area and approached the group at the monitor. Falc thought to tactfully test the waters, but instead blurted out, "So...what happened to all the furs and spears?" Aiyanna sighed.

Rikkar, beard as wild as ever, turned from the scanner to shoot them both an incredulous look. "We're certainly not going to finish it with a spear. I know you're a new recruit, but did you hit your head on the ice or something?"

"You still don't think you've ever seen either of us before?"

"Why would we have?" Rikkar looked to the others.

"So what - you don't remember what happened to Maple? Being taken by that thing into the ice?"

Rikkar quickly looked away to the scanner. "Anyone taken by the Jiekna quickly becomes part of the lake...."

"She was your friend and – " Falc quickly bit his tongue, eyeing Deliza, who he could tell was thinking hard, as if trying to recall an all-important but lost detail, brain jostled somehow by Maple's mention, but neural connections misfiring.

"So... we better get back to work, right?" Falc tried to change the subject, feeling guilt at any rate for bringing Maple up around Deliza. Aiyanna more tactfully approached her father. "So, Dakotah, how is the plan going?"

Dakotah grinned confidently. "Very well, new recruit. Hope you're ready for your first outing."

"Have had some good practice I think..." Aiyanna bit her lip. "But I really do miss my family. You must too, being out on the hunt so long?"

Dakotah exhaled and shot her a warm, wistful look. "You have no idea."

Falc tried to work his way over to Rikkar, but Deliza pulled him aside to a monitor, which displayed a spinning animated 3D model. "Welcome, recruit! Keep in mind, there are more than twelve different types of ice on earth and in the known universe. Dang, right? Some are actually man-made in the lab, but this one..." She glared in fasciation and tapped the hexagonally-shaped framework on the screen almost affectionately. "Has hydrogen bonding make up unlike anything I've ever seen before..."

Falc nodded, only partially paying attention as she continued, and he studied his grandpa's behavior at the scanner wall.

Deliza leaned in sarcastically. "Kid? Am I... boring you?"

Rikkar intensely tapped a metal rod against the floor. "Bundle up, everyone! The Sonar Frequency Fish Finder just picked up significant activity in sector 7. That's our starting point." He tapped a lake location on the map, not far from where they currently were. "New recruits, your value to the success of

56

this mission can't be understated."

Aiyanna nodded, playing along, comforted by the simple familiarity of seeing her dad. Rikkar proceeded to lay out specifics of the plan, which the more Falc heard of it the less he liked, especially with what his role psychotically entailed. All he could think of was how to snap his grandpa and the others out of this. Could they somehow push them back through the portal physically? Could everyone somehow make it back through one portal at the same time? They'd have to wait for opportunities but until then...

Within the hour, Rikkar, Falc, Aiyanna, Dakotah, and Slash were back on the ice, heading to "Sector 7". A sleet storm pounded them. Deliza stayed behind to run support from the tech ops center. They trudged forward in huge, hooded parkas, goggles, and loaded to the gills with augers, heat rods, and scuba gear strapped to a sled. Falc wiped falling snow from his goggles with a gloved hand, watching his grandpa stride purposefully forward. He was so different from when he saw him last in "Neanderthal man" mode but still had that same unfamiliar wild-eyed glare as Falc slid up next to him.

"So, why do we need to kill the Jiekna?"

"Survival, right? Between me or it, it's going be it." Rikkar muttered under his breath about "home" as he stomped ahead. Falc and Aiyanna were left trying to figure out the nature of where they were.

Aiyanna tossed out, "Is this really even them, or some kind of avatar or projection?"

"If nothing else, it seems each reality is some sort of manifestation connected to each shanty... or the people from it?

Before long they arrived at a single, rectangular ice hole, four by six feet wide. Rikkar checked in with Deliza, touching his comms headset, bellowing loudly through the wind and sleet, "We made it; how we looking?"

Deliza's voice over the headset responded, "Hear you. We're seeing only a spattering of activity, so they may have just dang straight moved on."

"Still, let's try to draw it out into the open." Rikkar proceeded to holler back to Dakotah, who immediately went to the sled and began prepping scuba gear. Goggles up, Falc used both hands to shield his face from pounding snow. How could he possibly have agreed to what they were about to do?! Was it because

Aiyanna had been there, had already been assigned her duties, and he didn't want to seem like a wimp? Was it because he didn't want her dad going it alone? Was it for Grandpa? All he knew was, all that gut-wrenching, mind and body-numbing fear he felt that day he saw the boy under the ice... was flooding back times ten. He. Was. Actually. Going. Scuba Diving. Down there!

Falc did a replay in his mind of just how *insane* the multi-pronged plan actually was. Rikkar, Slash, and Aiyanna would continue atop the ice, guided by the comm center's sonar tracking system. Falc watched Dakotah prepping the oxygen tanks... He and Dakotah had the insane task of shadowing the "Above Team" but underwater, continuing the pursuit in the void below. Dakotah handed Falc one of the ultrasonic fish deterrent rods, all part of the plan to "sandwich" the Jiekna from above and below using painful audio frequencies, pure speculation as to if it would even work. *It just keeps getting better!* Falc pondered.

Dakotah and Falc donned their fins, masks, and orb-like deep-sea helmets he'd never seen anything like over their thick wetsuits and masks. Dakotah tested the "dive torch," and a large underwater flashlight. He handed Falc two long, metallic rods and gave him an encouraging glance.

"Remember, just keep an eye out for the ice-phants."

"Which are?"

Dakotah smiled, trying to help calm his nerves. "Short for ice phantoms. Heralds of sorts. We can do this, just one step at a time, got it?" Falc nodded, thinking back to his only other diving experience, during summer vacation to Barkley Sound in British Columbia. *Fish sightseeing. Better than nothing, right?* Falc worked to convince himself of this.

"Wait!" Aiyanna suddenly rushed over to Dakotah, saying one simple Ojibwe word, "Ingodoode," as she touched his dangling necklace.

Dakotah stared at her inquisitively. "One family? How did you know...?" She flipped the oak pendant over: "Ingodoode" was etched into the wood. She tucked it into his wetsuit. "Just didn't want you to lose that down there." She gave Dakotah a big bear hug. He staggered back a few feet, again confused by the random gesture but clearly feeling some visceral connection. Next, Aiyanna turned and gave Falc a more awkward hug and whispered, "Take care of each other down there, hear me?"

Falc reddened. "Likewise up here. Not sure which is worse."

Dakotah gave a thumbs-up to Rikkar, adjusted his deep-sea diving grade helmet and vanished into the hole. Falc clicked on his helmet, grasped his ultrasonic rod, and crept closer to the edge. Nearby with a hammer, Slash pounded a spike into the ice and connected a neon yellow eighty-five-foot rope. Rikkar tightened the other end to Falc's belt as Aiyanna watched nervously. Falc mused about how her terrified expression pretty much captured how he felt at this point. Rikkar gave an assuring nod as he put a hand to his shoulder. "All set... Remember, these waters course through your bones too." Falc only had a split second to return a curious glance before Rikkar gave him a two-handed push in.

SPOOOSHHH! Falc submerged. Underwater, he entered a world of fluorescent murky hues blurring downward into blackness. He felt completely... altered. A full immersion intergalactic space travel virtual reality game he'd messed around with came to his mind for a split second, but only as a pale comparison. This was sensory overload, the ice cover ceiling overhead completely throwing off his sense of orientation and balance – he saw two "grounds" to walk on... as he viewed the lake bottom – *which is which? He wondered if he was upside down or right side up?* Falc began waffling and flailing about, nearing panic attack mode, which he had no idea was not uncommon for first-time ice divers.

"Recruit?" Falc's headset sputtered with Rikkar's voice. Falc continued to spin about akimbo, losing it. He could see Dakotah up ahead, turning perhaps to help.

"Recruit, can you hear me?" Falc floundered in darkness now. *What's happening? Does the Jiekna have me?* He wondered.

"Falc?" Rikkar's familiarity resonated in his mind. *Grandpa? Is it really you? Is this over?*

Falc finally forced his mouth to utter, "I'm here."

"Okay, this is Rikkar. Try to control your breathing... and I need you to watch your bubbles." Falc lurched sideways, now upside down, his light flashing toward the vegetation at the bottom of the lake.

"Bubbles?"

"Right, bubbles only go to the surface. Follow the bubbles up to the ice. You'll see us through the ice. We'll move together as one, understand?"

With forced resolve, Falc reoriented in the nocturnal waters to his rising bubbles. He fishtailed around and stroked his way upward... light growing... working his way toward the ice sheet and the water against it, which moved like magic mercury or bubbles blown through circular toy sticks. From underneath, Falc was suddenly seized by the ice cover's beauty and peacefulness.

####

Fifteen minutes later, Aiyanna, Rikkar, and Slash continued on above ice, the maelstrom lessened into snow flurries and lighter wind. Deliza had checked in over headsets with both teams but had no new information.

"What are we going to do if we find it?" Aiyanna asked.

Rikkar smiled a sly grin and reached for his backpack to remove an auger in one motion, wielding the power tool with its long, twisted metal drill like a cowboy pulling a shotgun. "We introduce it to six high alloy carbon steel blades and auger its frozen brains out."

Aiyanna glanced down into the ice, seeing the neon yellow rope underneath, signifying Dakotah and Falc were with them. When she glanced up, ice fishing shanties astonishingly dotted the horizon ahead, at least twenty. It was a whole different shantytown. "Whose are those?"

Rikkar mused, irritable. "The other ice fisherfolk."

"There's someone else out here? From town?"

"Maybe, maybe not," Rikkar said cryptically.

Slash peered about carefully. "They're from a not so nice off-ice place. Trying to throw us off the Jiekna's trail. They worship da thing like a god or something. My money is on these being decoy shanties anywho."

Aiyanna also noticed scattered carved ice holes in shapes ranging from stars to triangles and octagons. Simple wooden fishing poles were set hovering over each opening. "Any reason to worry about what they're fishing for here?"

"Best not to be worrying right now," Rikkar muttered, pushing out ahead.

On approach, Aiyanna noticed just how strange these shanties were. Some were of the standard variety wood construction, but others... were made of intertwined tree vines and branches, or plants like a natural outgrowth into intricately formed tiny shelters. Another was made of pure packed snow, like a picture-perfect Christmas sculpture. Yet, others were constructed of garbage dump-like refuse or jagged mountain stone, which were hard to imagine making it out onto the lake ice.

"Let's get the checks done," Rikkar directed, then adjusted his headset, speaking to Falc and Dakotah, "Below Team, hold up and standby."

"Mr. Rikkar, what exactly are we looking for?" Aiyanna followed up.

Slash set aside her backpack. "The more of us it kills, the more it can 'reflect' temporarily out into other dimensions. But full-on exit or re-entry can only happen through one special shanty somewhere out here on the ice, a sort of "traveling tele-shanty."

Rikkar piped in, "From what we can gather, that shanty shifts with the wind, with the storms, here one minute, gone the next. If the Jiekna finds it before we do, it can go other places, do who knows what. These other shanties are set up to make it difficult for us to find the exit way."

"But when we do find it, we torch bomb the entire shanty!" Slash made an exploding sound effect. "Boom, no more portal."

Rikkar motioned. "Let's get cracking. If the shanty inside has an ice hole with the same light pattern as the one you came through..."

"You mean that ultra-blinding extreme green glow weirdness?"

"That's the one. Could be here, may not be." Rikkar motioned her and Slash towards the shanties, assigning each a row to quickly investigate. Aiyanna approached her row. The first shanty was of generic wooden variety, nothing special in appearance. Over her headset she heard Slash, who must have been already leaving a shanty, simply state, "Clear." Rikkar quickly followed with a "clear" of his own. Aiyanna popped open her first shanty door, its steel handle cold from a layer of frost. The wooden structure was empty except for an ordinary round circle cut in the middle of the floor shedding soft blue light. She moved on.

Twenty minutes later, together they had knocked out close to thirty shanties.

Aiyanna approached an intricate "tree shanty" she had named on the fly and thought was an approp name. Its intertwining branch siding didn't appear constructed at all, but somehow rooted and grown from the ice, which of course she knew was completely illogical. She pulled back the door... tiny streams of light stretched across the structure, crisscrossing over a round, trunk-like opening in the ice. Aiyanna entered, examining the insides, a bit mesmerized... before slipping - SPLASH!

Aiyanna emerged from the water right away. *Oh my gosh? Did I just plunge back home? Where am I now, some other dimension?* The walls were different, made of cast iron, with a wood stove up on the ice nearby. Aiyanna tried to float horizontally first, then up, elbow-elbow, knee-knee, inching up on and out of the water. In a panic, she burst out the door, to see... open ice as far as the eye could see.

She heard a distant cry... Turning, she saw a tiny figure amongst a cluster of shanties two hundred yards away... it was where she'd just been. It was Rikkar! She carefully strode out over the slippery ice toward him, leaving the isolated iron shanty.

He yelled out to her, "I forgot to tell you. Some shanties built here have... different qualities. You go in one, you come out in another somewhere else across the ice. These are more run-of-the-mill tele-shanty. Not the ones we're looking for though!"

"Run of the mill... really?" Aiyanna shook her head at everything wrong with that statement, and sure wishing she'd known that ahead of time. After a walk back, she arrived at her row and next shanty to check. Aiyanna took a deep breath before entering, determined to be much more careful. This one had a fluttering white sheet instead of a door. She reached to brush it aside, her balance suddenly going haywire, as she plummeted face-first downward... She exhaled, catching herself on her forearms before her face hit the packed snow. Aiyanna glanced both ways to see she was on the open ice between several shanties. "Oh come on!" she exclaimed, exasperated. Rikkar emerged from another shanty, putting out a hand for her.

"Not your fault. Another thing I probably should have mentioned, some are a sort of Fata Morgana on steroids. Crazy thing, I tell ya." Rikkar exclaimed.

"Meaning?" Aiyanna blurted from the ice, exasperated.

"Ice Mirages." Slash giggled a bit.

13

FROM ABOVE & BELOW

An ounce calmer but still on complete edge underwater, Falc saw the Above Team's humanoid shapes up through the ice. He wondered what could be taking so long? Dakotah was in the lead, swimming a few feet ahead of him, shining his flashlight. Below, Falc's light evaporated into the abyss. Aiyanna had also checked in with them with an update on the shanties above. Falc could hear the concern in her voice for her dad, and also maybe just a bit for him too beyond the "concerned acquaintance" he wanted to think.

Falc decided it may be now or never and spoke into his comms headset within his helmet, "Grandpa – I mean Rikkar – are you there?"

"Copy that, what is it, recruit? You see something?" Falc heard Rikkar's voice crackle through his headset, breath panting from the above ice pilgrimage.

"No... I just... want to... need to... report a case of dereliction of duty." Falc bit his lip inside the helmet, awaiting a response. The silence seemed to stretch out like the endless sheet of lake ice itself.

"This isn't the military, son. And now is not the time for confessionals. Keep alert down there. We're almost done checking shanties up here."

"This may be my last chance."

"Fine. Who did what?"

"It was me. I wasn't there for... another member of the team. I was so wrapped up in daily stuff... logistics. In what I was running after, I lost connection. Critical part of the deal, you know?"

"Well, I'd say you're in it right now."

"And it's dang scary."

"That's natural. You're underwater searching for an ice beast."

"No. I'm more scared of losing - what we had."

"There's always time, now let's stay focused –"

"I'm sorry. I should have been there!" Falc blurted out.

"I really just need you to stay focused on the mission, recruit."

"Believe me, I'm fully engaged now. I'm just worried it's too late to make it right." Falc saw lights in the distance... like dozens of tiny lanterns emerging in the night. "I see something," he reported to Rikkar. Spectral lights were forming off in the grey haze.

"Hear it coming up here too... the lake ice keening."

Underwater, Dakotah pointed. Like a bloom of fluorescent jellyfish, the ice-phants emerged from the blackness, humanoid-shaped thin sheets of floating discolored ice, shifting in size and thickness, each reflecting echoes of a person, oscillating through their entire life cycle. Falc's eyes darted about, catching a glimpse of a man in an aristocratic 19th century-style suit, an ER nurse, a twenty-something punk rocker with a mohawk...Deliza's voice came over his headset, "Under Team, what are you seeing down there? Are the ice-phants within range?" Falc was swept up in this vision, watching their mouths move in unison as if in a chant, which underwater Falc and Dakotah weren't privy to hear, but somehow was producing sound waves which reverberated against the ice overhead.

Falc was shaken from his trance by Rikkar on his headset. "Means it must be close!" Falc could hear the lake ice's moans and twangs secondhand through his headset, "Rikkar? Aiyanna??" His only reply was the secondhand splintering of lake ice overhead. He had at least temporarily lost contact. *They just can't hear because of all the noise*, Falc told himself. *They're okay.*

A dozen phantoms broke from the group upwards toward the ice, mouths accelerating, speeding up the rhythm of their keening song. CRACK! TWANG!

MOOAAN! Spread out, those banshees merged into the white above, becoming one with the connecting ice cover - RHHHZHHHIT! To Falc, the entire lake seemed to shake. Cracks and fissures shoot out like earthquake fault lines across the ice above them. Scattered holes exploded upward, sucking water and ice back inward. The ice-phants were now within feet of Falc and Dakotah.

Suddenly they were engulfed by them, like a bloom of amorphous, fluorescent jellyfish, the mortified Falc and Dakotah drifted among the ice-phants. They crowded and inadvertently bumped into Falc in passing. Each touch sent a charged chill through Falc. Before his eyes, the small ice form of a ponytailed girl in a parka grinned at him; she morphed quickly, ice expanding in size with her into a large woman with fiery red hair in a flannel pajama onesie... It was Maple!!

She reached out to him, expression befuddled and scared. Falc jerked back. Maple shrunk into an elderly woman before his eyes, and then to ash set in black ice... Falc gazed in awe through her empty canvas and the flowing watery void beyond. She reversed course, transformed from crone to younger woman in seconds, toward childhood as she drifted off. Falc watched in amazement, struck with sympathy and interest in these life stories encapsulated in ice drifting past, stuck in uncertainty on how to feel – sad, scared, or both. For a moment, he stopped trying to rationalize the wonder of any of what he was seeing.

Amidst the reflective echoes, he saw Dakotah a few feet away, who gave him a thumbs-up. "They're like living histories!" he uttered through his headset gleefully. The final wave of ice-phants swam past them, receding away into the depths like a school of sturgeon.

Falc's headset crackled to life, Deliza blurting, "All right, team, we have a reading, it's coming your way fast!" Falc felt like he should say something to Deliza, but as usual, couldn't find the right words... What *could* he or anyone say?

####

While frantically working through the final few shanties, Above Team heard

Deliza's message loud and clear. Rikkar, Aiyanna, and Slash all quickly emerged from shanties simultaneously, eyeing the final shanty, twenty feet away. Aiyanna eyed the rectangular boxed shanty, which seemed to recede into the icy field, thick moss covering much of its wooden structure.

The ice below rumbled, spitting snow in the air thirty feet away. They whirled toward the encroaching Jiekna, barreling directly for them! Rikkar quickly spoke to Falc via headset, "Below Team, ready the ultrasonic rods!" He pulled the auger from his pack and powered it up, blades spinning furiously. Aiyanna removed her ice pick; Slash her toothed saw. *This was it.*

"Come to me, Jiekna," Rikkar issued, challenging the very ice itself.

Underwater, Falc and Dakotah tracked the Jiekna's malleable silhouette, its vague impression gliding inside the ice, in and around ice bubbles, streaking for them or toward the final shanty and ultimate escape. They stroked and kicked their way as close up against the ice sheet as possible, raising their ultrasonic rods to it... Heads nearly touching the ice, Falc's eyes grew bigger as he stared horizontally across the ice at the encroaching powerhouse. Reverberating ice shards sprayed downward into the water in its wake...

"Twenty feet... 15... 10..." Dakotah reported through his headset to Below Team. "Now!" Falc and Dakotah clicked on their deterrent rods, plastic tips lighting up red, activating the 2000 hz high-frequency waves, not hearable to humans. In the ice, the shape of the Jiekna suddenly came to an absolute standstill nearly atop them. Its crystalline coyote head wildly bit down into the water.

On the surface, a pair of jagged ice claws had emerged upward around Aiyanna and Rikkar but were momentarily paralyzed. Rikkar raised and drove the spinning, twirling auger down into the ice like a Viking berserker with an ax, its blades whirling into the Jiekna's midsection, like a corkscrew into cork. Ice chunks and flurries spit into the air. The Jiekna's upward bear face writhed in agony.

Underwater, Falc and Dakotah simultaneously watched its downward coyote head seizing in fury. Ice tentacles shot out, extending into the lake to flail at them; Dakotah and Falc instinctively angled away. Two tentacles slid by. Falc returned his focus to the ice cover overhead, seeing the augur blade grinding in the ice above as the Jiekna convulsed. On their headsets, they heard Rikkar grunting and screaming as he forced the blades downward.

Suddenly, the ice tentacles doubled back, slapping the deterrent rods from both of their hands. Dakotah swiped at his rod before it was sucked into the depths by a watery vortex. Overhead, the Jiekna jerked around, its snarling ursine head now focused, bending its shape around the auger to break free. It scuttled away down the ice. Falc heard Rikkar cry on his headset, "No, it's on the run!"

Dakotah had drifted away a bit, directly in the Jiekna's escape path. Falc screamed, "Mr. Baikie, watch out!" It seemed to unfold in slow motion underwater... the Jiekna's ice head dipping below, morphing from the ice cover, its giant, gaping, top-of-head maw swallowing up Dakotah in one continuous motion, without breaking its fluid stride. Falc froze, blood running cold.

Falc heard Aiyanna's voice, "Dad, you okay?" Falc's heart sank, mind catastrophically falling apart. *This was all his fault. Why didn't he stop this insane plan? Straighten Grandpa out? Why didn't he say something from the beginning? What could he say to...*

"Falc? Is my dad alright?" A long pause. "Say something!!!"

Falc floundered, not realizing he was swimming as hard as he could after Dakotah.

"Aiyanna, I -" was all he could mutter.

"Dad!!!!!" echoed panic-stricken Aiyanna in his headset.

Falc stroked uselessly after him, watching the icy impression of the Jiekna vanish in the distance, slithering off with its prey through the ice cover bubbles, to the sound of Aiyanna's soul-crushing cries.

14

SHANTY LOGIC, SHANTY RULES

.

Aiyanna burst through the door of the Tech Trailer, followed by the others. "You still haven't given me a straight answer, Rikkar, where does it take them!?" Close behind, Falc gasped for breath, still in his scuba gear. *Dakotah, Maple*, he wanted to tell Deliza...

"I'm sorry, he's simply lost. There's nothing we can do," Rikkar stated, flummoxed.

"That's crap!" Aiyanna pushed past Deliza, trying to control her emotions. "Maybe there's a way we can save him back in our world?"

"Exactly, we all gotta go back!" Falc pleaded.

Rikkar folded his arms and shook his head regretfully. "The mission."

Aiyanna threw her hands up in desperate frustration and raced further back into the trailer. Falc followed her past the monitors and stored scuba gear to where he knew they were going... the ice hole portal.

####

Understandably, Aiyanna wasn't there to help him out of the water this time. Bobbing in the ice hole water, Falc caught sight of her—wetsuit and all—momentarily as she raced out of the Tech Trailer shanty. Falc struggled to climb out and hightailed it after. She was already at her shanty by the time Falc pushed through the swinging Tech Trailer door outside. He glanced around at *their world* for a moment, the other shanties and a vague visual of town through a now thicker mist, as he stepped out into slushy water up to his ankles. *Meltwater was pooling everywhere atop the ice.* Falc swallowed hard, considering what this meant: a preternaturally fast "ice off."

As he sloshed through the water toward her shanty, his mom and dad came to mind. He thought for an instant how he missed them, that they had to be searching soon after he didn't come home, could bring help...

Entering the shanty, Falc found Aiyanna kneeling at Dakotah's frozen figure. He was prone on the ground alongside the iced-over fishing hole portal, just like they found Maple. Aiyanna was frantically feeling for a pulse, the wrist, his neck. Falc tried his wrist for a pulse. "Is there a faint one? Maybe? I can't tell!" she uttered, glancing up to Falc teary-eyed. He nodded and jumped to her side as they began in with CPR... Falc pumped the chest 123... Aiyanna delivered a breath, chest 123, breath, chest 123 breath... they kept at it working... working. Aiyanna's expression grew more desperate; Falc wished he didn't feel so helpless, could bring him back, stop her pain... After a while, they just sat there, not moving from their positions, Falc atop Dakotah, Aiyanna whimpering and crying, holding her father's head in her lap.

"Maybe if we get him to a hospital right away..." she muttered.

Falc exhaled, wondering if the time was right. "I have to tell you something. Could be important. I saw Maple..."

"What do you mean?"

"Under the ice. She was an... ice-phant or whatever they called them. Came right up..." He whipped his hand past his face. "Recognized me."

"What did she look like?" Aiyanna wiped snot from her nose, trying to get her breathing under control.

"She was scared."

"Then they're alive somehow. The Jiekna must be able to undo this."

Falc looked away, racked with guilt. "I'm sorry I couldn't help - it just happened so fast."

Aiyanna leaped to her feet. "Not for another second, Falc. It's what we do next that counts."

Falc tried to smile but couldn't quite muster it up. He remembered Aiyanna's dad talking like that in class, something about being "creative in each new moment." He quickly laid out his other big concern, "I don't know how time is correlating between worlds, but here it seems to still be the same morning we left, despite the days it seems like we've been spending through the portals."

"So....?"

"The ice cover melt is somehow hyper-accelerated. The ice shantytown is sinking - it may only be a matter of hours. What's happening on the other side must somehow be accelerating the ice off. This will all be gone - "

" - Then we really need to get to that next shanty portal," Aiyanna tried to process.

Falc supportively nodded. "Let's go."

She gratefully reached out a hand to help him up, watching her dad the whole time. They clasped each other at the elbows, like two warriors psyching each other up for battle. Aiyanna took things one step further. "But we need to hit Tech Trailer first."

15

SLASH'S INSULATED ICE SHELTER

The day before, the FishTech 1000 Hub Ice Shelter with its polyester thermal shell and aluminum poling leaned against a shed wall compacted into its six-foot-long backpack case behind "Slash's Phantasmagoria." The darkened store was filled upfront with wondrous wood-carved critters and creatures: bears, raccoons, wolves, mastodons, and bucks. Across the street at Earl's, Slash was cozying up to the bar, downing another happy hour bottled beer. Several empty bottles stood in front of her. And so the days went. She was in one of her funks. This one was bad, worse than the others. She hadn't been able to carve anything in weeks. And if another dude tried to hit on her, she would literally smash every one of those bottles against his skull and gouge his eyes out. No joke.

Her backwoods brother back home in Wisconsin always called it "Carver's Block" with a sneer. What he didn't understand, couldn't understand was how she poured her heart and soul into every carve, how high it made her and how it killed her to stagnate. An out-of-place tourist in a preppy jacket across the bar tried to make eye contact with her. I dare you, Slash thought. Come on over. In a daze, she pushed away from the bar in disgust and yelled across the bar to him, "Sparing you a world of hurt, trust me." Seconds later she was out front into the arctic air. Like that, she ended up horizontally in the air, a rookie mistake, an ice slip with feet flying out in front followed by landing hard on her tailbone. Slash rolled in pain onto her stomach,

touching the ice. Grimace turned to an epiphany. She pounded her fists against the ice giddily, breaking through her mental block as mildly curious Yoopers watched through Earl's front window.

The two wetsuit garbed teens re-emerged into Slash's shelter from another ice hole inside. Aiyanna hefted a black sea sack up onto the ice, which they had gathered from the Tech Trailer for this portal adventure. True to form, the portal in the Tech Trailer had been iced over after being used for entry and exit, just like her shanty. *One roundtrip plunge per person per shanty,* Falc surmised about using the "shanty logic" they were cataloging. They discussed what that meant with only two more shanties, meaning after this one, they only had one more shot to somehow help the others and figure things out. They had also made a quick pitstop to Grandpa Rikkar's shanty for Falc before jumping into the ice hole in Slash's shanty.

Pulling themselves up out of the portal's watery depths with the ice claw, they immediately saw new "chainsaw art," basically mini sculptures built from parts and a broken open case of Northern Star brown beer, which they hadn't seen on the other side.

"Where is everyone when you need them? Aren't we always greeted in some salty way?" Aiyanna spouted in annoyance. Before long, they popped open the door and were back on the ice.... the field of whiteness stretching out before them in an empty void, no signs of life. "Hello?" Falc ventured out.

Aiyanna followed more forcefully, "We're the new recruits, don't you know?! We're here!" At first, they were so opaque they almost missed them. Standing by where the fire circle had been in their reality, were seven standing lifelike ice sculptures erected in a circle of defensive action poses, like mythic superheroes. It was the remaining group... Rikkar, Slash, Deliza, as well as them. Aiyanna and Falc approached and walked among them, examining their incredibly lifelike features and similarities. Falc went closer, examining Aiyanna's statue, and the intricate individual fingers pointing into the distance, an ice pick in one hand. Slash's statue consisted of two gleaming and jagged chainsaw-like arm extensions raised overhead. The Rikkar sculpture leaned back in a primal yell to the sky. Falc's sculpture was posed like it was running in the other

73

direction.

"Slash's work." Aiyanna immediately thought.

"One would think, coming through her shanty, but who knows at this point." Falc kneeled and identified vague, bizarre prints in the ultra-thin layer of snow over the ice, almost like hooves. The tracks dissipated a few feet off. He reached into the sea sack Aiyanna had brought, producing a handheld portable "fish finder" device. He fiddled with turning it on. Aiyanna sighed, reaching over to help. "Click here for fish... here for lake bottom contour... water depth... is right there. See?"

Falc nodded. "Thanks. Grandpa saw these as cheating, so I never used them."

"Uh-huh, right. Maybe we'll get lucky and stumble onto it. Where do you think everyone else is?"

"My guess is back out on the hunt again too."

They trekked out onto the sea of ice, direction uncertain on the open expanse. Every few minutes Falc checked his watch, turning to keep an eye on Slash's shanty behind them. He wondered about the nature of time there... *Shouldn't someone be looking for them from back home by now?* Clearly, their last few visits had taken up at least entire days, but it was hard to tell. The ice had a way of *melding time, like floating under the ice in darkness with no orientation...*

"I'm so stupid," Aiyanna blurted out.

"What are you talking about?" Falc suddenly felt bad for being lost in his own thoughts.

"The things I wasted time on." She glared out over the ice toward the grey horizon.

"I get it."

"Nah, don't think you do at all."

"I mean your dad... To be honest, I've always... thought you had it figured out... had the primo life hack or something. This is gonna sound weird, but you're just... bona fide."

Aiyanna smiled a little at the compliment, shook her head, and stifled back tears. "I just see I could have been more caring, more connected... not just to Dad, but with other people... It's as clear as all this." She waved at the ice.

"It's part of the reason we took this trip since my parents' separation."

"Oh geez, didn't know. Sorry."

"But that's just it, we're not growing apart, I'm just growing up. I've seen it coming for ages, and the crazy thing is which I know is against how everyone tells me I'm supposed to feel, but they are happier apart. Which means I'm happy for them."

"Wow, that's new."

"Not that it's been easy. Part of you wants things to stay the same, but they just can't forever, eh?"

Falc gave her hand a little squeeze. "I'm not gonna give up here, so you know." She shot an appreciative glance. "Let's find them."

Later as they moved across the ice, nightfall began to cast a dark haze, shrinking their field of view seemingly by the moment. The fish finder suddenly began shrieking like a party of four-year-olds seeing a birthday cake. Falc pointed the finder directly down to the ice, trying to get a reading on the digital contour map. Aiyanna looked heartened, just at the thought of finding anything. The bleeping weakened, which instantly struck Falc as odd. Aiyanna reached for the Fish Finder and helped Falc raise it upward to point out across the ice...

Through the darkening mist, dozens of shanties were revealed speckled across the horizon. This ice fishing shantytown was definitely similar to the one Aiyanna had seen before she mused, with a variety of constructed shanties, from wood to stone and steel. Open ice fishing holes with wooden tip-ups with lines attached were also scattered about.

"Careful, all or some could be ice mirages. Been there," Aiyana warned. Suddenly a whistling filled the air as snow flurries began to swirl down from every direction. Cocking their ears about, they tried to find the sound source... but it seemed to be everywhere at once. Cautiously approaching the first row of shanties, they peered around town. No one in sight... but the howling whistle grew and echoed, more like a tune melodically rising and falling as the flurries thickened. They peeked around a wooden shanty seemingly constructed from water-grooved driftwood. The melody seemed to hover on the wind, ethereal and otherworldly.

75

Around the next row of shanties, they saw... a crowd of at least twenty figures sitting in thick, hooded parkas as white as the snow-covered ice which supported their collective weight. In front, children sat before a tall, shirtless man, which was shocking considering Falc and Aiyanna both consistently saw their own frigid breath billowing before them. The man's long, stringy, white hair almost touched the ground, face a deep, wrinkled brown as he played a flute made of ice... or bone, the clear source of the melody... the howling whistle they heard. The falling snow intensified.

Falc noticed it first. Shapes were moving twenty feet in the sky above the crowd. Vague impressions, figures, like stick figures in particles of sand. Amidst the falling flurries, a story with apparitions was unfolding in the air above them as dozens of virtual Jieknas maneuvered on the stage in the sky, over a ghostly ice cover-like surface. From their angled vantage point, Falc and Aiyanna looked upward to watch, as if through a hollow plateau from a desert below. The Jieknas came in all shapes and sizes, with a multitude of icy facial structures from earthy animals to shifting otherworldly gaseous gargoyles, ranging from the mundane to monstrous, bobbing up over and down under their ice sheet in the sky domain. Falc wondered, was the flute-player some sort of Shaman, musician, or storyteller? Or all three combined?

Along with the off-icers including children in parkas, Aiyanna and Falc stared in wonderment at the holographic-like collage of snow, ice crystals, and starry sky. Suddenly, a discordant sound erupted from the flute, like bones horribly snapping over and over. The ice sheet in the sky brittly shattered, sending the Jieknas sporadically dropping from their perch. Aiyanna and Falc covered their ears, a grinding sound seeming to emit from the sky story itself. The off-icers watching wailed in agony. A wave of thick snow blanketed down to wipe the scene of the Jieknas clean, dissolving to a visual of a giant floating ice hole portal, which filled up the entire sky.

In the sky story, creatures, with their multifaceted monstrous faces, plummeted out of the portals and down into hovering lakes. Several Jiekna reversed course and rose back up to ram against the portal, which was now solid ice and denying entrance. Then, the portals shrank and disappeared. Humanoid figures were walking on the sky ice everywhere. Falc and Aiyanna continued to watch the story, recognizing one group which grew larger than the others. It was Rikkar and the company atop the sky ice cover. Bursts of snow like laser beams fired back and forth between the group and a Jiekna, who floated below in mortal combat. The Jiekna began sucking each figure one by one down through the sky ice, each vanishing into its translucent, pulsating form. The portal reappeared and began to grow with each absorption...

Aiyanna heard another voice suddenly. Falc spun to see fifteen feet away, a rogue off-icer emerging from a shanty with a thin, ebony sword-like blade. He made startling eye contact with Falc. The flute stopped cold. In a tongue neither of them could understand, unfriendly voices clamored.

16

TELE-SHANTIES

Aiyanna and Falc were backtracking in a heartbeat. They dodged between shanties, trying to stay out of sight, crouching behind another, waiting for an opening...

"Come on," she whispered.

The shadows from off-icers stretched out in front of them. Then behind. Both left and right... Aiyanna nudged Falc quietly through a small door into a wooden shanty. Purple, wavy light shifting back and forth illuminated the barren wood panels, emanating from a circular ice hole.

"They'll find us for sure in here," Falc muttered.

Aiyanna grinned. "Just what I was hoping for, it's a tele-shanty."

"A what?"

"Yup. Just what it sounds like."

"Thank you, world, for wetsuits." Falc tried to smile back as she took his hand and together, they took the plunge. SPLASH!

A moment later they sprang back up and used their ice claws to pull out of the portal. They had indeed teleported; this shanty was full of crates packed with fish in ice. "Let's get moving." Falc hurled the wooden door open and without thinking took a few steps outside... right into the central gathering area, interrupting thirty off-icers listening to the storyteller's next tale. They collectively whirled to him angrily.

Sleet pelted Falc in the face as he realized the tele-shanty had taken them directly into the center of the ice shantytown. He gulped. "Not good..." He whirled around to reenter the shanty, but a hulking off-icer had already snuck behind, placing a hand on the door and angling it shut, glaring at him. Falc bolted off between two shanties to create a diversion, screaming, "Go back through, Aiyanna!"

The storyteller screamed something incomprehensible to Falc. He darted between off-icers, but had become encircled fast... *Another shanty is the last option!* Falc dove through the door of a yellow-painted wooden shanty, an off-icer grabbing his foot. Falc shook free, climbed into the watery portal and fully submerged, hoping for the best.

He emerged seconds later, bobbing in the water with all thoughts on Aiyanna. *How was he going to find her again? What was he thinking just walking out like that? He had to be more on point!* He was now looking at a different shanty thankfully, which meant he'd gone through another tele-shanty. *But what if they followed him? Would they do that?* He used his ice claw to pull himself out. The interior decor was fairly bare, containing a pile of bowls, moccasins in various stages of being sewn together, and a pile of aged books. He suddenly heard heated voices outside and froze. A rumbling followed. Sunlight streamed inside, slipping between the panel's nooks and crannies. He sat on the edge of the ice hole... *Should he go back?* He heard a hand turn the doorknob. Falc tensed, gripping the slippery edge...

"New recruit! I wondered where you'd gotten to. Where's your partner?" Rikkar stared at him expectantly, garbed in a thick lumberjack coat, jeans, and a black skull cap over his ears. Falc guffawed.

"Grandpa - I mean - Rikkar!" Falc gushed, jumping up to his grandpa as the latter backed out of the door. He rushed his grandpa, expression a complex mix of joy and sadness. "I get it, you've never seen me before, right? Don't care right now, I'm giving you a hug anyways." For a millisecond, Falc remembered how when he was little, Grandpa used to sweep him up into a giant bear hug, his cinder block-sized hands gripping him lovingly.

"Better think again, recruit!" Rikkar held him off. "Don't go all melodramatic on me. The hunt is on and..."

"Yes, yes, I get it, you need me focused, right?" Falc flashed a somber smile. "Well, ya, now you're getting it."

Falc saw beyond Rikkar, and his jaw dropped. Slash and Deliza stood aboard a serious state-of-the-art on-ice vehicle. It was a crimson-colored hovercraft with a Kevlar hull, carbon fiber body and black skirt material around its base like a Navy SEAL assault ship, packed with modified chainsaws, flame throwers, plexiglass shields and what looked like several small cannons. Slash, garbed in a black bomber jacket and sunglasses, jumped from the hovercraft. and let out a wolf-like howl,

"ARRRRRUUHHHHHRRRR!!!" She approached with some kind of barbed contraption in one hand.

"Hey, new guy, you know how to use these?" She held up her glove, which actually was the contraption, jagged metallic edge and all. Falc shook his head, a little scared. "I don't even know what that is."

"Well, you need to know both." She suddenly spun and karate chopped cleanly downward into the ice with her free hand, her chainsaw-glove blade slicing neatly into the ice - RHHHHROOOOOO! The blade started to cut a circle around him as she moved. Slash pulled up next to Falc and cut the motor.

"Now you try this one." She tossed him the other contraption, literally a combined long ax with a chainsaw head. Falc fumbled to catch it without cutting himself and thinking, *who tosses chainsaws?* Falc saw the ripcord and eyed her. She shot him a "What are you waiting for?" look. He thought, *Guess no safety training, huh?* He yanked on the cord: nothing. He chuckled nervously. "Happens to me with the lawnmower too." She stared obliviously at him.

"Lawnmower?"

"Forget it. Here we go again." The second time was a charm. It revved to life, seeming to tug Falc forward from the starting momentum. He grabbed it with two hands to steady himself. She pointed to the ice. Falc screamed into the crisp air, which he had to admit felt kind of good, as he chopped down into the ice, splitting a crack open much deeper than he imagined it would. He tried to carefully pull it back, nearly falling over as he flipped it off.

"Not bad. I'll teach you the chainsaw cannon later." Slash nodded.

"You made all this stuff..." Falc shook his head. Slash beamed.

Before long, they were all in the hovercraft, skirting across the ice. Deliza scanned the ice with binoculars while Slash drove. Falc was astonished at its speed, maybe forty or fifty miles an hour? They smoothly scooted across the frozen tundra, in and out of open pockets of water stretching as long as thirty feet. Falc thought nervously, *What does this mean for our shanties and the ice back home?* He had to *"flip the script" on the whole hunting trip fast.* Rikkar had explained to Falc they had a line on the Jiekna escape shanty and were hightailing it there. Falc marveled at the assortment of chainsaw themed weaponry set in racks along the passenger seats. For a third time in as many minutes, Falc tried to bring up his biggest worry. "What about Aiyanna? We've got to find her."

"She went through training like you, right? Then she can take care of herself on the ice. Maybe we'll pick her up along the way."

Falc unzipped his wetsuit exterior pocket and set a tiny, wooden box on Rikkar's lap. Rikkar instantly questioned, "What's this? Too small for any kind of useful tool or weapon."

"Just take a look," Falc replied. Rikkar did. He popped open the hand-held pinewood box, then looked surprised. He grasped the first yellowing and ripped photo. It was of a much younger Falc, maybe five or six years old, in snow leggings and a heavy down jacket standing on snow patch-covered ice with a grinning Rikkar. Falc held up a small lake trout horizontally with both of his little hands, gleaming with pride, his self-proclaimed greatest catch of all time back then. In the photo, a younger Rikkar stood equally proud sharing the moment, his arm lovingly around Falc's shoulders.

"That was the big one for me," Falc recollected fondly.

In the hovercraft, Rikkar thumbed through other photos bewildered... he and Falc's mother, more with Falc...

"Where did these come from?"

"Our home. Where we both came from." Falc pointed at the picture wistfully. "I just wish I could talk to that Rikkar again."

"This... You are strange." Rikkar glared in confusion.

"That version of Rikkar had a disease... and it's as if that disease just vomited across dimensions to here, dragging everyone in its icy wake with it."

"But that's me...How did you make these? How did you even think to do this thing?" Rikkar touched an unexpected tear rolling down his face; he tried to shake off a bodily reaction he couldn't connect a reason to.

"Don't know what to do with that emotion, do you?" Falc countered. Rikkar concentrated on the photos harder, as if flipping through them faster would clarify them.

"Why does killing the Jiekna mean so much to you? Would it help somehow?" Falc inquired.

"It's always been there, right beneath us, and we didn't even know it. To it, we are some kind of mythic creatures, and as such, sometimes it's up to such beings to set things right. If we don't deal with it now, no one can ever go where they need to. Do you see that?

"I'm trying to, I really am."

"No, I literally mean, look!"

Slash veered wildly, leaning against her instrument panel. "Escape shanty ahead! But we're not solo!" Further ahead, a sea of thirty off-icers were striding toward them, swords drawn. Equal distance away, a lone shanty was covered in mist.

"Recruit, Deliza, prep the cannons!"

"You want me to fire chainsaws or something at them? Aiyanna could be their captive!"

"No, stupid, just use the ice cannon on them! We don't want to kill THEM."

"Jiekna!" Deliza screamed. At three o'clock from their six o'clock, ice shot into the air as the impression of the creature could be seen hurling through the ice cover. It was barreling directly for the shanty. Rikkar's eyes went wide. "We have to stop it!!!"

Falc jumped behind the rectangular-shaped ice cannon. Thick sheets of ice, each the size of a small desktop, were loaded and stacked like cartridges into the cannon's back. Suddenly, the hovercraft was in the middle of screaming off-icers swinging axes and swords at them.

"Sorry for this!" Falc hit the trigger and worked the throttle. Ice-munitions fired like a machine gun, slabs flying to pelt off-icers, driving two and three at a time back into each other.

Rikkar hooted and hollered, "Way to go, rookie!!!"

The hovercraft split through the crowd of off-icers, leaving them in the dust, and spun to a stop at the shanty ahead of the Jiekna. The team leaped out, each loaded with their choice of weapon as they fanned out around the shanty. "All right, everyone, protect the portal and let's take it down!" The Jiekna closed in, an impression barely visible in the ice, faint spray firing into the air in its wake.

"Watch it! Fire at will!" The Jiekna circled them, twenty yards away in the ice, one... two... three times. Then, it rose from the ice, its multi-directional monstrous face glaring at them, frozen eerily still back into its statue mode. KA-POW! An explosion erupted from Rikkar's chainsaw-canon. The mini chainsaw hurled through the air, blades spinning, CRACKITY CRACK CRACK!!! The Jiekna tried to duck, but the saw caught its right hawk face, shattering it into ice shards! It shrieked in pain and dove back into the ice. Rikkar quickly hefted up the flame thrower and laid out a layer of fire across the surface. Steam rose from the black ice. "Now!"

Slash leaped forward with a battle cry and attacked up its side with the chainsaw sword and glove, digging into the ice. Deliza and Falc both followed up the other side around it, yanking the cords of their chainsaw pickaxes. Falc drove his downward, cutting into ice. The Jiekna groaned and cracked in response. Rikkar eyed the ice with his flame thrower, laying out short spurts directly in front of him. "We're hurting it!"

Intense cracking suddenly filled the air around them in every direction. Their world turned upside down; the literal ice cover itself lifted and tilted at a sixty-degree angle, knocking everyone to the ground. They slid downward toward an open water hole, near the side of the escape shanty, which had begun flickering in and out of existence.

"The shanty's about to shift! We've got to stop it now before it gets in!" Slash screamed.

The ice sheet slammed back down, slapping the lake water. Closest, Slash unsheathed two chainsaw swords, ran forward, then jumped and slid across the ice to arrive before the shanty. "Come and get it, brah!" Slash hollered as she rose, a Jiekna claw rising simultaneously before her. Slash screamed, driving both chainsaws into it, spewing ice chunks into the air. Multiple Jiekna ice faces on spikes suddenly shot up before Rikkar, Deliza, and Falc, like some arctic medusa. Slash made short work of the ice claw, cutting it clean... not noticing the fourth head rising behind her... Falc saw the shanty flicker one more time and vanish from sight.

The Jiekna's head expanded and bit down on Slash. She yanked against its head momentarily trying to pry free... "Bring it – "

Then Slash was gone.

"Slash!" Falc yelled, slicing at the Jiekna face in front of him. Nearby, Rikkar busily melted the fourth face with the flamethrower - which was shrieking and dissipating much slower than any ice had the right to.

Falc whirled to see Deliza being taken too! He revved his chainsaw and rushed forward... A tentacle slapped him across the face, forcing him to tumble, feeling blood pool inside his jaw. Then a cylinder of ice clamped down on him, enveloping his view.

17

BEYOND COLD

F alc realized he had been swallowed into the Jiekna's head. Encased in ice, he was sliding just beneath the surface and picking up speed. The ice around him moaned, groaned, and croaked, elongated cries which seemed to echo and reverberate back into him, like a rubber band made of sound snapping back and phasing against his veins. The cacophony accelerated, the freefall turning into a vertical descent, becoming dizzying, disorienting as frozen ice bubbles and shapes hurled past his vision. Falc was unable to move or respond as if dragged face-first along white concrete, which was twisting and grooving into him. The motion began to melt away into a blank opaqueness. He was unsure if he was moving anymore, as unthinkably cold ice pressed down against his face and body, literally growing and eating at him... as the inside of his eyelids iced up. The loose blood mixed with saliva in his mouth was freezing solid.

The cracking effects morphed into a steady howling, echoing wind. The cold became subzero, accelerating by tenths quickly. His mind sputtered like a skipping song, then entered into the emptiness inside those skips. Falc began to sense a crystalline ancientness that was the ice... He felt himself transforming... his very cells icing... into something else entirely. Was he imagining this part, he wondered? Or was he part of what he saw - the only visual now in his perception, a rolling hill of cosmic ice on some distant, otherworldly place... maybe a planet? Moving and stationary he felt at the same time, Falc understood somehow this was dwelling beyond time and space... the past, present and future integrated simultaneously in multitudes. Three moons and the light from a sea of stars reflected off his cosmic ice, and at the core, he felt part of something so enormous, so unimaginable... Amplified groaning-moaning, twanging, and popping of the ice followed, which it was clear was now coming from him/it/all - the core. It was as if he could sense the ice in collective reflection, but beyond any concepts of language or light. Then, shafts of illumination cast rays from the void to generate a small amount of heat on his frigid surface. SPLASH! In a flash, he was suddenly back underwater, floating with the keening horde of frost phantoms, ice-phants beckoning him closer...

18

HEATED UNCERTAINTY

F alc opened his eyes; he saw Aiyanna's brunette hair draped over his face an inch away. She suddenly jerked back in panic, from delivering mouth to mouth. "Holy shit, you scared me. You're alive!" He coughed violently, water pouring from his mouth... as if he'd been underwater. "You're okay?" Falc croaked weakly, shivering... "Heat."

"Huh?" Aiyanna responded.

Falc's mind felt like it had been through a blender as he rambled, "Your heat."

"Easy there, big guy."

"No, what makes molecules move, time flow. The entropy that drives... the free fall center into the uncertainty of it all... okay, I'll shut up," he rambled, unsure why.

Aiyanna watched him, concerned. "You're welcome, if that's some bizarre thank you. Now we have to move!" Falc stared at her; Aiyanna had a large cut across her forehead and scrapes on her face. They were in Slash's shanty.

"What happened?"

She helped him to the door; Falc was aghast at what he saw. Due to the melting ice, the Tech Trailer's nose was partially underwater - CRACK CRACK! Slash's shanty they had been in suddenly shifted downward, slipping halfway underwater. The entire little ice shantytown was under siege by the lake, with every shanty in some stage of submersion. The roof of Aiyanna's shanty leaned against the ice cover, nearly completely lost to the lake.

Grandpa Rikkar's truck "Bessie" had been driven and was near Slash's shanty, two wheels submerged under cracked ice.

"Come on!" Aiyanna yelled, pushing them to jockey across the most solid ice they could find, still a few feet deep in the meltwater.

"How did you get back... your dad?" Falc mustered up.

"We're sinking here, so the super short version as we go." Aiyanna explained how she'd found an off-icer's parka in the shanty after they separated, blended in temporarily with the group just long enough to escape. After looking for him, she eventually worked her way back to Slash's shanty where she thought he might also backtrack too. Eventually, she decided to go back through the portal for help. "I decided to try and drag my dad and Maple on the sled to our truck in the parking lot. Of course, we had a little run in with the Jiekna first. Long story short, we ended up ramming your grandpa's car through the Jiekna ice sculpture, which really seemed to piss it off!" Falc for some reason heard the shattering and ice explosion in his mind.

"Cranked up the heater to Papa's truck and..." Aiyanna shook her head in disbelief.

"Are they?" Falc asked, still processing her epically impressive solo battle with the Jiekna while he navigated the ice cracking between his feet.

She smiled. "Unfreezing frogs, right?" Falc remembered what he had said earlier. Somehow, they began to slowly come to, in a similar fashion.

"Shanty rules, shanty logic. Then why are you still here?" Falc practically yelled, slipping on ice.

"I couldn't just leave you behind, idiot. Figured I could still come through using your last shanty portal. I was about to, then you showed, literally your body icing up really fast." He tried to explain what happened to him, which he found was pretty impossible to put into words. They decided somehow he was transforming into one of the Jiekna's underwater ice-phants, and she interrupted the process via CPR just in time before he drifted away. The whole experience left him shaken, unsure of who he was, even more than usual, if that were possible. They hurried to Grandpa's shanty, which was tilted down into the water at a twenty-degree angle.

"Deliza, Slash... they must be back now in their shanties," Falc uttered desperately. "Can you get them with the sleds too?"

Aiyanna understood what this meant, that he was going back for his grandpa through the final shanty, when Falc read her mind. "What about the fifth shanty?

"We still don't know whose it is. I tried to pry the door open again, no luck." They entered Grandpa's shanty, Aiyanna immediately noticing the painted walls. The water's green light illuminating the painted ice field matched the real one outside, the arctic forest with snow-covered trees on another wall, and moss-colored moon against a starry sky on the third. "Woah," she said.

"I know, right?" Falc said as he stuffed several items into a backpacking sea sack and zipped it up. He moved toward the portal, shyly saying, "Would I be out of line if..."

She grabbed and kissed him awkwardly as they moved. "How seamless was that?"

"Nice move."

"You taste like... hypothermia."

"Go figure." He waved and jumped in.

19

THE FISHERMAN'S SHANTY

The afternoon before, the ramshackle shanty had rested lifelessly in the backyard, snow climbing its walls and melding it into a drift. Inside the single wide sectional home a few feet away, Rikkar rushed through his kitchen on a mission. Shouldn't Earl be picking him up for work soon? Very strange for him to be so late. He considered whether maybe he should get his jacket on. When was the last time he'd been on the job? Rikkar wondered where his dad was and why Falc hadn't visited in so long. He played with that name for a minute... Falc.... but for some reason couldn't put a face to the name. Instead, he visualized the comic book art panels in his studio. Rikkar had been thinking he drew those himself and was quite proud of them. He sniffed the air. Nasty. Literal crap. Could that be coming from him?

He thought for sure he had made it to the bathroom this time. That "little woman" who kept showing up had been making him wear what he called, "those dang space diapers." Was she his mother? Rikkar thought to call her but couldn't remember the number or where he had written it down. He glanced back out into his yard. His mind locked on the majestic ice fishing shanty snowdrift. A lucid idea struck him like a buck against the windshield. Pantless and shoeless, he pushed open his back door, answering the call.

Falc emerged from the water into a starry skied darkness, which he quickly realized stretched in every direction. Night had fallen in ice shanty land. The four sides of Grandpa Rikkar's shanty were there but lying flat on the ice, having collapsed outward. Probably not a good sign, he decided immediately. *Had the Jiekna attacked Grandpa here and knocked them down?* Falc climbed out and removed his sea sack, which contained among other emergency items, a flashlight. He shined it in a full circle around him. "Grandpa? You out there?" He paused, sighed, and tried again, yelling, "Rikkar!? Hello?" Nothing. The light's beam seemed to die about twenty feet away as if the very ice sheet itself fell off the face of the earth. He noticed the ice felt uneven, as he teetered on his feet.

In his field of vision a few feet away... there was a small fishing hole with a large tackle box, wooden rods, and a five-pronged ice spear lying by. Falc cautiously approached. He gave another quick glance about, then popped open the "Big Alvin's Shop" brand tacklebox. It reclined back into three levels, revealing an assortment of brightly colored lures of varying sizes and shapes, glittering metal and wood, along with spools of line. There was also... a note. Falc unfolded it and read:

New Recruit,

To catch up with the excursion, fish. Be sure to set the dang decoy. Will wanna us the thick line.

Big R

Falc blinked in frustration. He whirled around, talking to the air as if it was Rikkar, "Are you kidding me? There's no time, Grandpa! We're going to be underwater anytime!!!" He sighed and reconsidered. *What other options are there? Have to find him. This could be some kind of trigger in this reality.* He rummaged deeper in the large tackle box, finding a "grandpa special" as he called them, wrapped in a towel. The carved wooden decoy was shaped like a fat walleye, expertly crafted, top fin protruding down the fish's back like a mohawk with giant eyes and lips. But it was the coloring that made it

Grandpa's masterpiece, Falc thought. It was as if an intergalactic supernova had exploded from its guts, reverberating cosmic hues of reds, blues, and purples out across its body. There was something else. There was a small box containing three tiny, thin sticks, which were either flares or some sort of dynamite, he decided. *You've got to be kidding me.* Falc shook his head. *What was Grandpa... Rikkar up to now?*

As illogical as it was, he set about following the letter. Finding several slats of wood at the bottom of the tackle box, he began to build a tip up. Before long, he had crafted the wooden scaffolded structure, which stood a foot high and reached over the ice hole. He attached the "supernova fish decoy" using the hefty fourteen-gauge marine wire, just like his grandpa had taught him. He moved the spear to the edge of the water. He decided to double down and also drop a lure, finding Grandpa's Chubby Billy Rattle jib on a spool, via a clinch knot, passing the line through the hook, doubling it back, twisting it over and over and on he went...When finished, he did what fishermen do, he insanely sat there, despite knowing the ice was collapsing by the second back home. *If the shanties sink before they can get back through...*

Falc watched Supernova Fish Decoy and began to talk to it, "Hi, Rikkar. You won't know me... I fully get that now... and I guess dwelling in the past is pretty pointless too." Falc stared for long moments down into the green-hued water.

"I also understand that you won't leave until we've caught the big one - the Jiekna." Falc sighed. "Why am I talking to a decoy like it's you?" The decoy's fat lip bobbed up toward him from underwater. Then, Falc did the exact opposite of what he thought he should. He sat down on the ice, trying to calm his mind and body, watching the decoy, the water... as he fell into a meditative state. For the second time in his life and possibly on the same day, he lost time and himself. Minutes, hours, maybe days passed? He was unsure. He only knew the overlap of the oscillating waters, the ice, and his grandpa's bobbing supernova fish decoy.

Below in the water, a distant dot came into view under the decoy, breaking his trance. It climbed from the depths, quickly growing faster and faster - SWOOSH! The tip up flag hurled upward...

"Harold!?"

The gigantic silver fish he saw back through Dakotah's shanty portal swallowed up the decoy in its mouth and veered away. Falc's eyes went big, and he saw the marine gauge wire go taut. He grabbed the spear... and suddenly the ice itself rocked as if being tugged. Falc fell on his butt hard. "Ouuffff!" He tried to stand, but rollercoaster-like vertigo kept him from righting himself. Then the ruckus suddenly stopped. Complete silence.

The sky had turned a twilight golden glow now, and he could see he was actually on a small ice floe, floating in the lake. There were ice floes everywhere on open water, drifting and colliding like floating puzzle pieces that didn't quite fit. Jagged floes ranged in size from a few feet wide to a few hundred, some with icy hilltops, undulating trails, or crystalline forests of seeming ice, all constantly shifting in disorienting fashion. Falc considered, *If this reality was breaking up like this, what does that mean for the lake back home?* He again imagined momentarily the sinking shanties vanishing into the icy waters. They had to be gone by now. He prayed Aiyanna and the others were making it out at least. He tried to not think of his mom and dad, where they were in all of this and what they must be thinking. Time here seemed to be flying...

He took in the sky again, now seeing an incandescent greenish moon surrounded by starry wave patterns like subtle lake waves undulating above water. He recognized it instantly as Grandpa's wall shanty painting Aiyanna had literally just been gawking at. *As before on his other trips, somehow this ice dimension had pulled from Grandpa's psyche parts of its design.*

THUNK! A floe collided with the one he rode. On the neighboring floe, which contained rolling hills of ice: footprints. The floe bobbed and began to rotate away... Falc grabbed the tackle box and spear and jumped aboard, following the prints. He examined them as he went, no doubt Colster Boots which made deep impressions and were clearly Grandpa's. *I don't know where he is, but I can finish the job for him. Then he'll come back,* Falc thought determinedly. He carefully tracked the prints across the puzzle piece floes, losing them at various times as they shifted. After a few more hours, Falc feared he'd permanently lost them, so he jumped across a small lake gap to a floe containing what appeared to curve up to a hilly pinnacle of ice. At that point, he felt it was as good as any way to go.

As soon as he landed on the floe, he saw prints somehow manifest up ahead, and he continued pursuit. The wind whipped up intensely, chilling him further. Before long, sleet and snow joined into a swirling, greying storm. Falc briefly contemplated his near "ice" experience which Aiyanna saved him from, and just how completely lost he felt... *Who and what am I at this point? I don't know.* Falc shook such thoughts off and tried to stay focused on the tracks, one step at a time, using the spear as a walking stick. Bizarrely, the tracks seemed to appear and disappear sporadically as he braced against the wind. Snow and sleet pelted him, creeping into the nooks and cracks between his gloves to his wrists, which he relentlessly tried to shake out.

He was suddenly struck with his singular mission now: finding and killing the Jiekna. The temperature was clearly dropping as he felt his feet and hands going numb. He lost the tracks, found them, then stepped into the tracks. They were his exact size. Was he going in circles? Was he going insane? Ice crystals felt glued to his eyelids. *Oh no.* He glared around, frustrated, but could only see a few feet ahead.

He trudged forward in the maelstrom, now a snow-covered figure melding into the scenery. His mind drifted to the idea that maybe he actually was his grandpa all along, *my footprint fit right?* Maybe that's who he was all along... why he so clearly saw what needed to be done now.

Falc tried to clear his head when he noticed some sort of man-made structure ahead, which at first glance appeared to be growing out of a snowdrift. As he approached, he realized it wasn't a shanty or snow cave, but a small, kid-sized lean-to with three sloped sides like a tent. The lean-to was constructed from tree branches that had long been frozen over, generating an eerie post-apocalyptic effect. Falc circled the lean-to first, thinking about getting out of the storm for a minute. He pried back a few branches and climbed into the frosty hut. Inside, he was surprised to find an old wooden fishing pole and a boy's-sized parka, hard as a block of ice. There was also a small pile of stacked wood, Inuit-style. In the corner, he found a small tin box. He dusted it off, blowing snow away. Inside, there was a small drawing pad. He flipped through the sketches, all images of the ice he'd just traversed, including the green moon and undulating sky. *They're pretty good*, Falc pondered.

####

Thirty minutes later, Falc continued on, still in a virtual white-out. Without footprints to follow, he aimlessly climbed up and over ice boulders which stacked twenty feet high. Had to keep going. One foot in front of the other. It all seemed endless. It seemed like he had been on the ice one way or another for so long... He had been looking for patterns in the fissures and cracks to follow, but they all looked the same.

He remembered Dakotah and Deliza and how they studied the ice... they were trackers somehow. Falc fell limp onto the ice. It felt good to him to be down on all fours. He put his bare hands out over the translucent surface, drawing his face closer to touch the coldness of the surface. From there, he could see drifts of snow spread out around him. This was a new perspective that didn't seem to scare him anymore. He concentrated... and noticed a vague protrusion up from the ice. He saw another swell. Then another mound. He crawled after them... then stood up, feeling more confident. They were inverted track impressions, on the underside of the ice... Now he was the tracker.

Minutes later, he climbed over a jagged boulder. Atop it, he peered down and froze. Across a watery field of scattered ice floes, each 10 to 30 feet wide, the lichen and moss-covered escape shanty floated by itself on a singular floe!

Falc picked up the pace, digging in the tacklebox for the explosive charges. *Why not just destroy the shanty once and for all? Maybe that's what Grandpa had in mind?* Then he saw it again. The Jiekna was on another ice floe, floating closer to the escape shanty, but separated by water it apparently couldn't pass through. The ice beast shifted around on the floe, eyeing the shanty like a pit viper waiting to strike. Falc knew he had to do it for Grandpa. *It may have already gotten him... That was the least he could do!*

He clicked the activation button on the explosive sticks, the only thing he imagined to do with the explosive. The button gleamed red. Falc instinctively hurled the two in a rapid-fire approach, one as far as he could hurl it from there out in front of the Jiekna, the other to its side to veer it away from the shanty. Ice shards and water exploded in every direction on contact. Falc stared shocked at their effectiveness and the display. When the spraying

95

cleared, he strained to look, searching... The Jiekna had survived and was on a smaller floe, further isolated but still floating toward the escape shanty. Falc dropped the tacklebox and leaped with the spear, nimbly jumping from floe to flow, closing in to finish the job.

This is it. If he kills it, we can go back home. He landed on the ice floe next to the Jiekna, spear raised. A thin ice tentacle struggled to rise up a few feet out of the Jiekna. *If he killed it, Grandpa would be like he was before. They'd be buds again the way they used to be. Things would be the same...*

Falc knew things would never be the same again.

He glared at the thing. On the tiny ice block, the Jiekna seemed so small now, no bigger than a dog. Its coyote head lifted skyward, spraying ice crystals like a cough. Eight feet away, the escape shanty skipped a beat, visually phasing in and out of existence. Time was running out for the creature to slip through, whether to our world or another. Falc was suddenly overwhelmed with emotion, remembering Grandpa, the lake waters, the ice... the Jiekna... This was the endgame.

The hike back to the portal was somehow longer, but that may have been because Falc dreaded what he knew was coming next. He blocked sunlight from his eyes with a glove as he saw a figure by the shanty portal. Falc approached to find Rikkar, who was gazing off as he sat on the edge of the ice hole, dangling his knees casually down into the frigid water. Rikkar casually called out, "Hey there, recruit."

"Hi, Rikkar. Aren't you a little cold?"

Rikkar smirked for a moment. "You know, the world doesn't have ice, the ice has the world in it, right?"

"Makes sense," Falc responded, arriving directly across the hole from Rikkar.

"Anything to report?"

Falc's voice quivered. "Yes. I freed it. I let the Jiekna go."

Rikkar eyed him squarely, not speaking for some time. "That's quite a thing to do." Rikkar took a deep breath, suddenly growing emotional, Falc sensing something almost like pride. Rikkar pointed to the water.

"Something I couldn't have done." Rikkar lingered in the moment, leaning back to eye the stars. "Lots of lakes out there for it. All kinds of seasons." Falc wanted to just stay there a bit longer now, but he knew... Rikkar turned to him directly.

"Time to go then."

"Right," Falc responded sheepishly.

"Do you want me to tell you I'll be right behind you, would that help?"

"No, I know you're not coming back with me."

Rikkar eyed him with the gleaming certainty of a solitary owl's stare. "This is where I want to be now."

"But that was some adventure, eh?" Falc said, eyes tearing up.

Rikkar smiled. "How about we agree to call it our first... and last adventure together?"

"Deal."

Rikkar nodded. "Then we won't count the time we killed that tub of Blue Moon ice cream together."

"You remember?" Falc glared, astonished.

Grandpa Rikkar just smiled back, his whole figure seeming to shimmer in the reflected sunlight off the ice.

"The excursion is over for me. People make a big deal about memory. How will you be remembered in years to come, a legacy, etc... but regardless of if anyone can remember jack in twenty or eighty years or a millennia from now, it doesn't mean we didn't happen. We did, we do, and dang spankin' always will."

Falc nodded, fighting back the swelling feelings inside. He watched as Grandpa turned sideways... to reveal he was already a two-dimensional ice-phant, a literal phantom of ice.

Rikkar dunked into the water for a moment. Falc watched as Rikkar's form morphed and shifted, aging into dust on the pane, then back again to the little boy he saw under the ice the day he himself first had the incident on the ice, before this all started.

Rikkar rose to the surface again, holding the form of the twelve-year-old boy momentarily. "Time, as you know, is perceived differently here. So, in a way, I've always been here and there since I first came. Sometimes impressions sneak over a bit. That day, part of me saw you above the ice...somehow in my excitement, I busted up, didn't mean to scare you. Just missed and wanted to chat with you."

Falc kneeled at the edge, fighting back waves of emotion. "I'm glad you did."

"You'll always know where to find me, Wingo." Grandpa uttered his final human utterances before submerging one last time before Falc.

20

ICE OFF, ICE ON

F alc emerged from the ice hole a final time, chilled literally to the bone, locking eyes in recognition with a Grandpa Rikkar "original" carved owl bopper passing by in the water. It was in motion, sliding directly at him, he ducked sideways, pulling himself up onto knee-deep partial ice sheets. The backside of the ice shanty was collapsing into the lake, two-thirds underwater!

Crawling out and hurling the door open, Falc had to shield his eyes from the bright sunlight. The lake was a bustle of activity, sinking ice floes and shanties. Two police rescue hovercrafts bobbed in the water and on ice floes at the other mostly sunken shanties. Falc saw Aiyanna wrapped in thermal blankets aboard one craft, breath ghosting. Falc tried to yelp out to her. An officer on the boat pointed toward him from thirty yards away. Falc saw the Tech Trailer shanty hanging on by a hair to an ice flow with its back two wheels in the air, the rest swallowed up by the lake. Deliza was similarly huddled on the other boat looking shocked. Slash was being fished out of the icy waters, shivering and reaching back toward the dark void teary-eyed. "My saws, no, please God, why?" The little ice shantytown was only a memory now, Falc thought. And Grandpa... Suddenly he saw Aiyanna on her feet eyeing Falc, arguing with a policeman vehemently while pointing.

THWOCK! Falc turned toward the sound... a burly policeman in another hovercraft was taking an ax to the front door of the fifth shanty. "Hello, anybody in there?" A third of the shanty was cockeyed down into the water. TWOCK- TWOCK! The door gave way into several brittle pieces; Falc exhaled, wincing in anticipation of what would come next. The policeman took a confused step away, fumbling onto his backside against ice.

All activity seemed to freeze as everyone viewed the fifth shanty's occupant. Inside was Slash's original ice sculpture creation: the mythical creature with its curved, levitating wave trunk, humanoid torso, spear-like arms, and four-fold hollow skull with twisted expressions facing in every direction. It was the creature known to the inhabitants of the small ice shantytown as the Jiekna. Falc squinted to take a closer look... Each face was different now, not animalistic as before, instead there was Slash, Dakota, and Deliza's icy visages on the different sides of the head he could see.

CRACK-CRACK! The shanty suddenly shifted, sinking further sideways, its roof sliding partially off. Sunlight reflected through the Jiekna's head ice and cracks; its audience watched, collectively bewildered by the singular sculptured head with its connected faces. *Is it, are they moving?* Falc stared at the Jiekna, sensing its presence; he knew it was really there. Did it tilt - or nod? - toward him in recognition? The Jiekna suddenly dove or sank, depending on the perspective angle or belief, as the entire shanty vanished beneath the ice.

Then the hovercraft was there... Falc climbed aboard. Such normalcy, such reality, other people, all of it feeling surreal and unreal to him. Two police parted, and his mom was there on the boat, swallowing him up in a maternal embrace, muttering about him not coming home the night before and the search... It had all happened only overnight... *Time, Time, Time,* Falc thought, so fluid, so bendable. Eventually, she simply said, "Grandpa?" When Falc finally opened his eyes, he saw Grandpa again and pointed.

On the ice, just beyond where the fifth shanty had been vanquished, his familiar figure was there. It was the legendary scene of Grandpa Rikkar in his tiny chair, slumped over the perfectly round cut fishing hole, revealing the secrets of the lake he loved to his core. He held his fishing rod steady, line dangling in the water.

The hovercraft approached, and a policeman wearing fishing leg gaiters jumped out onto the ice sheet and sloshed toward him through meltwater. The officer pulled up as he closed in. Glanced back uncertain for a moment. He checked the pulse of the frosted figure; Falc already knew the answer to that one. His mom whimpered, deep and guttural. The policeman simply stared back at them, fear in his eyes. Falc hugged his mom tightly.

He stared at the permanent expression of serenity etched on his grandpa's face and smiled. Another policeman aboard whispered under his breath, "How macabre."

Falc pulled away from his mom and looked squarely into her heartbroken eyes. "Remember the little boy I told you about who was lost under the ice?" His mom searched his eyes, trying to understand through her grief. "He made it back home... just like Grandpa."

On the hovercraft ride in, Falc worked his way over to Aiyanna. He learned Dakotah and Maple were already in the hospital and on the road to recovery, their memories coming back, which he was grateful to hear. They held hands for a minute, appreciating the shared warmth. "We're actually making it off," Falc considered.

"But let's keep testing the ice, okay?"

"In this metaphor, if we fall through together, is that a good or bad sign?"

Aiyanna shrugged as she took his hand again and they climbed ashore.

CRACK, SLEING, POW! PWEVV!!! A year later, Blackbird Lake once again moaned, groaned, and twanged its age-old sound show, echoing to the peak of Mount Tumbak. From there, the view rolling down to the lake revealed a tiny speck in the distant background, etched into the fabric of the landscape, a fine detail bringing the whole image to life. Falc, bundled up in his new green parka, sat on the black ice cover in the middle of the lake. It was now a ritual for him, after his own rite of passage. He now understood this to some degree. He took a sip of hot chocolate from his thermos and savored the extra whipped cream, just the way they always did. Falc watched his breath ghost and simply was present. He was part of this place now too, as a way to connect and be everything at once. It would be different every time, it would be their time together.

About the Author

Christian Raymond is an award-winning writer, media maker, film professor, and educational program developer for creatives. From auspicious beginnings as a seven-year-old hawking homemade comic books at a lemonade stand, his adventures have run the gamut from writing screenplays at Disney to designing collaborative digital storytelling projects with communities in Transylvania. He can often be found lost in the wilderness with a furry friend.

Made in the USA
Coppell, TX
22 March 2022

75399142R00066